The Sorrows of Young Werther
and
Novella

Johann Wolfgang von Goethe

The Sorrows
of Young Werther

and

Novella

Translated from the German by
ELIZABETH MAYER
and LOUISE BOGAN

Poems translated by W. H. AUDEN

Foreword by W. H. AUDEN

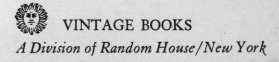 VINTAGE BOOKS

A Division of Random House/New York

VINTAGE BOOKS EDITION, November 1973

Library of Congress Cataloging in Publication Data

Goethe, Johann Wolfgang von, 1749–1832.
  The sorrows of young Werther, and Novella.

  Translation of Werther and Novelle.
  I. Goethe, Johann Wolfgang von, 1749–1832. Novelle.
English. 1973. II. Mayer, Elizabeth, tr.
III. Bogan, Louise, tr. IV. Auden, Wystan Hugh, 1907–
tr. V. Title.
  [PZ3.G552So4] [PT2027.W3] 833'.6 73–4285
  ISBN 0–394–71958–1

Manufactured in the United States of America

Contents

Foreword

So far as I know, Goethe was the first writer or artist to become a Public Celebrity. There had always been poets, painters and composers who were known to and revered by their fellow artists, but the general public, however much it may have admired their works, would not have dreamed of wishing to make their personal acquaintance. But, during the last twenty years or so of Goethe's life, a visit to Weimar and an audience with the Great Man was an essential item in the itinerary of any cultivated young man making his Grand Tour of Europe. His visitors in his old age were innumerable, but most of them had actually read only one book of his, written when he was twenty-four. What Goethe felt about this may be guessed from his first version of the Second Roman Elegy.

> Ask whom you will, I am safe from you now, you fair ladies and fine society gentlemen! "But did Werther really live? Did it all really happen like that? Which town has the right to boast of the lovely Lotte as its citizen?" Oh, how often I have cursed those foolish pages of mine which made my youthful sufferings public property! If Werther had been my brother and I had killed him, I could scarcely have been so persecuted by his avenging sorrowful ghost.

The biographers tell us that *Werther* was the product of Goethe's unhappy love for Charlotte Buff, but this is certainly an oversimplification. When writing a novel, an author naturally often makes use of his personal experiences, but a novel is not an autobiography. Goethe, for instance, did not, like his hero, commit suicide. Again, Goethe makes Werther an idle dilettante, who sketches a bit, reads a bit, but is incapable of seriously concentrating on anything. There is an element of self-portraiture in this: all his life, partly out of a temperamental impatience and partly because he was interested in so many things, he found it difficult to finish a work, but idleness was never one of his vices. When he wrote *Werther* he was probably in a disturbed state, for, a year after its publication, he wrote: "I am falling from one confusion into another." The novel seems to me to be one of those works of art in which the conscious and unconscious motives of the creator are at odds. Consciously, that is, Goethe approved of his hero, but his unconscious motive was therapeutic: by cultivating to the extreme, but only in words, the indulgence in subjective emotions typical of the *Sturm und Drang* movement, to get it out of his system and find his true poetic self, just as Byron, after *Childe Harold,* was able to put humorless gloom behind him and realize his true talent as a comic poet. Certainly, the admirers of *Werther* would have been bewildered by these lines written in Goethe's middle-age.

> *Vergebens werden ungebundne Geister*
> *Nach der Vollendung reiner Höhe streben.*

Wer Grosses will, muss sich zusammenraffen;
In der Beschränkung zeigt sich erst der Meister,
Und das Gesetz nur kann uns Freiheit geben.

(Unfettered spirits will aspire in vain to the pure heights of perfection. He who wills great things must gird up his loins; only in limitation is mastery revealed, and law alone can give us freedom.)

Living in the twentieth century, not the eighteenth, and knowing, as most of his contemporaries did not, Goethe's later work, *Werther* can still fascinate us, but in a very different way. To us it reads not as a tragic love story, but as a masterly and devastating portrait of a complete egoist, a spoiled brat, incapable of love because he cares for nobody and nothing but himself and having his way at whatever cost to others. The theme of the egoist who imagines himself to be a passionate lover evidently fascinated Goethe, for, thirty years later, he depicted a similar character in Edouard, the husband in *Elective Affinities*.

Had Goethe, from the bottom of his heart, really wanted his readers to admire Werther, why did he introduce the story of the servant who is in love with his widowed mistress? After nursing his love in secret for some time, he finally makes a pass at her, is surprised in the act by her brother and, of course, fired. Shortly afterwards, he shoots the servant who had taken his place, though he has no grounds whatsoever for supposing that the latter had succeeded where he had failed. Goethe not only introduces this character but also makes Werther, the future suicide, identify the murderer's situation with his own, thereby making it impossible for the reader to think of suicide as "noble." Again, if Goethe really wished us to be Werther's partisan in the erotic triangular situation Werther-Lotte-Albert, one would have expected him to make Albert a coarse philistine to whom Lotte is unhappily married, but he does not. Albert is, to be sure, a "square" who does not appreciate Klopstock or Ossian, but he is presented as a good man, affectionate, hard-working, a good provider, and Lotte as a contented wife. Never once does she show any signs of wishing she had married Werther instead. She is very fond of him, but evidently thinks of him as a "brother" with whom she can have interesting conversations. Her weakness, which is in part responsible for the final catastrophe, is a dislike of admitting disagreeable facts: she keeps on hoping that Werther will get over his passion and become just a good friend, when she should have realized that this would never happen, and that the only sensible thing for her to do was to show him the door.

To escape from his own emotional confusion, Goethe became a civil servant at the court of Weimar, where he soon had important responsibilities. Similarly, in a moment of lucidity, aided by the good advice of his friend Wilhelm, Werther realizes that the only sensible thing for him to do is to give Lotte up, go away, and take a job, also, apparently, as some sort of civil servant. The society he now finds himself in is stuffy, snobbish, and conventional, but the Count, his boss, takes a great liking to him, and he seems all set for a successful career. Then a disagreeable but trivial incident occurs.

[Count C.] had invited me for dinner at his house yesterday, on the very day when the whole aristocratic set, ladies and gentlemen, are accustomed to meet there late in the evening. I had completely forgotten this fact; and it also did not occur to me that subordinate officials like myself are not welcome on such occasions.

The "set" arrive and he senses that the atmosphere is chilly, but, instead of leaving, defiantly remains, is openly snubbed, and finally has to be asked by the Count to leave.

About this several things may be said. In the first place it is the professional duty of anyone in diplomacy or civil service not to forget the habits of the society in which he is living. Secondly, Werther is already well aware that the aristocratic set consider themselves superior to everyone else and, therefore, to himself, for he is not of aristocratic but bourgeois origins. Lastly, if a man thinks the social conventions of his time and place to be silly or wrong, there are two courses of behavior which will earn him an outsider's respect. Either he may keep his opinions to himself and observe the conventions with detached amusement, or he may deliberately break them for the pleasure of the shock he causes. He makes a scandal, but he enjoys it. Werther, by staying on when it is clear that his presence is unwelcome, defies the company, but his precious ego is hurt by their reactions, and he resigns from his post, returns to Lotte and disaster for all, destroying himself and ruining the lives of Lotte and Albert. What a horrid little monster!

* * *

Novella, published in 1828, four years before Goethe's death, is an excellent example of a literary genre, the idyll, at which German writers, more than those of any other language group, have always excelled. (I cannot think of a single English work which could be accurately classified as one.) It may be read as a postscript to one of his greatest masterpieces, the epic poem *Hermann und Dorothea,* published in 1798. Like the pastoral, the presupposition of the idyll is a harmonious relation between man and nature, desire and reason, but its descriptions of man and nature are much more realistic, less idealized, than those of the pastoral. An idyll, like a comedy, must end happily, but, unlike a comedy, it is always sober and serious.

In *Novella,* there are two significant locations, the town market and the old castle, and two types of human character, the huntsman and the trainer of wild animals. The market is an image for a good human society, peaceful, industrious, co-operative, prosperous.

> The Prince's father had lived long enough to see, and to put to good use, the day when it became clear that all the members of a state should spend their lives in the same industrious way; that everyone should work and produce according to his faculties, should first earn and then enjoy his living.
>
> . . .
>
> There were mountain people, having come down from their quiet homes among rocks, firs and pines, and mixing with the plains people, who lived among hills, field and meadows; also tradespeople from small towns, and others who had

assembled here. After having quietly surveyed the crowd, the Princess remarked to her companion how all these people, wherever they came from, used for their clothing more material than was necessary, more cloth and linen, more ribbon for trimming. "It seems to me that the women cannot pad themselves enough, nor the men puff themselves out enough to their satisfaction."

"And we won't begrudge them that pleasure," said the old gentleman. "People are happy, happiest indeed, when they can spend their surplus money on dressing themselves up and decking themselves out."

The old castle, long a ruin and overwhelmed by the forest, is now being repaired, not, it seems, to make it rehabitable, but as a tourist sight. If I understand Goethe rightly, he is telling a parable about the relation between wild, that is to say untamed, nature and human craft, or *techne*. Man must respect Nature and not try to enslave her: on the other hand, Nature needs Man's help if she is to realize her full potentialities. The daemonic, destructive aspect of Nature is represented in the story by the fire which, for the second time, has broken out in the market and threatens to destroy it. It is to be noticed, however, that a fire in such a place is probably caused by human carelessness: it is not an "Act of God." Man can and should tame Fire, just as, if he will have the sensitivity and the patience, he can tame the lion and the tiger. All too often, however, he regards wild creatures as things to be killed and exploited for his own pleasure. Significantly, in describing the Prince's hunting expedition, Goethe uses a military metaphor.

. . . the plan was to penetrate far into the mountains in order to harass the peaceful inhabitants of those forests by an unexpected invasion.

It is natural enough that the Princess should be scared when she sees the escaped tiger approaching and that Honorio should shoot it, though, as they are soon to learn, it would have done them no harm unless frightened. Honorio's second thoughts about his deed are more dubious.

"Give it the finishing stroke!" cried the Princess. "I'm afraid the beast may still hurt you with its claws."

"Excuse me, but it is already dead," the young man answered, "and I do not want to spoil its pelt which shall adorn your sledge next winter."

The same attitude is displayed by the castellan, who is annoyed that he cannot shoot the lion.

"Why did I take my gun to town yesterday to have it cleaned! If I had had it handy, the lion would not have stood up again; the skin would be mine, and I would have bragged about it all my life, and justly so!"

The Prince, the Princess, Honorio are good people but they are in need of further education, of the lesson in reverence for Life which is given them by the humble family, man, wife and boy, to whom the tiger and the lion belonged. Because they are good people, they are willing to learn even from their social inferiors. It was a fine artistic stroke on Goethe's part to make the chief instructor the child, and let him deliver his message in song, not in prose.

W. H. Auden

The Sorrows
of Young Werther

I have carefully collected and here present to you whatever facts I have been able to discover concerning the history of poor Werther, knowing that you will be grateful to me for doing so. You cannot withhold your admiration and love for his character, any more than your tears for his fate.

And you, noble soul who feels the same longing that he felt, take comfort from his suffering, and let this little book be your friend, when, because of destiny or some fault of your own, you cannot find a nearer and dearer one.

--*❧ Book One ❧*--

How happy I am to have come away! Dearest friend, how strange is the human heart! To leave you, one so dearly loved, from whom I was inseparable, and yet to be glad! I know you will forgive me. Were not all my other personal relationships definitely chosen by fate to torment a heart like mine? Poor Leonora! And yet I was blameless. Was it my fault that, while the capricious charms of her sister provided me with a pleasant entertainment, her poor heart built up a passion for me? Still—am I altogether blameless? Did I not encourage her emotions? Did I not relish her perfectly genuine and naïve expressions which so often made us laugh, although they were anything but amusing? Did I not—but oh, what is man that he dares so to complain of himself! Dear friend, I promise you I will improve. I will no longer ruminate, as I always used to do, on the petty troubles which Fate puts in my way. I will enjoy the present and let bygones be bygones. You are certainly right, best of friends, that there would be far less suffering in the world if human beings— God knows why they are made like that—did not use their imaginations so busily in recalling the memories of past misfortunes, instead of trying to bear an indifferent present.

Be so kind to tell my mother that I shall attend to her business as well as I can, and that I will give her news about it soon. I have seen my aunt, and found that she is far from being the disagreeable person my family makes her out to be. She is a lively, impetuous woman, but very warm-hearted. I explained to her my mother's complaint concerning that part of the legacy which had been withheld from her. She told me the reasons and motives of her own conduct, and also the terms on which she would be willing to hand over everything, and even more than we asked. In short, I do not like to write more about it just now; tell my mother that all will be well. And again I have found, handling this trifling piece of business, that misunderstandings and neglect create more confusion in this world than trickery and malice. At any rate, the last two are certainly much less frequent.

Otherwise, I am very happy here. The solitude in this heavenly place is sweet balm to my soul, and the youthful time of year warms with its abundance my often shuddering heart. Every tree, every hedge is a nosegay of blossoms; and one would wish to be turned into a cockchafer, to float about in that sea of fragrance and find in it all the nourishment one needs.

The town itself is not pleasant, but all around it Nature expands an inexpressible beauty. This moved the late Count M. to lay out a garden on one of the hills which, intersecting one another in the loveliest natural diversity, form the most charming valleys. The garden is simple, and as soon as one enters, one feels that it was planned not by a scientific gardener but by a sensitive heart wishing to commune with itself alone. I have already shed many a tear to the memory of its former owner, in the crumbling summerhouse which was once his favorite retreat, and now is mine. Soon I shall be the master of the garden; the gardener has taken to me after only a few days, and he will not fare badly.

May 10

A wonderful serenity fills my whole being, like these lovely mornings which I enjoy with all my heart. I am quite alone, and pleased with life in this countryside, which seems to have been created for souls like mine. I am so happy, dear friend, so completely sunk in the sensation of sheer being, that my art suffers. I could not draw anything just now, not a line, and yet I have never been a greater painter than at the present moment. When the mist rises around me from the lovely valley, and the sun at high noon rests on the roof of my impenetrably dark forest, and only single shafts of sunlight steal into the inner sanctuary, and I am lying in the tall grass by the falling brook, discovering the variety of thousands of different grasses closer to the ground; when I feel nearer to my heart the teeming little world among the grass blades, the innumerable, inscrutable shapes of all the tiny worms and insects, and feel the presence of the Almighty who created us in his image, the breath of the All-Loving who sustains us, floating in eternal bliss—my friend, when everything grows dim then before my eyes, and sky and earth rest in my soul like the image of a beloved being— I am often overcome by longing and by the thought: could you only breathe upon paper all that lives so full and warm within you, so that it might become the mirror of your soul, as your soul is the mirror of the infinite God! —My friend— but it is more than I can bear; I succumb to the power and the glory of these visions.

May 12

I do not know if mocking spirits haunt this place, or whether it is the warm heavenly fantasy in my own heart which transforms everything around me into a paradise. Near the entrance to the town is a fountain, a fountain which holds me spellbound like Melusine with her sisters. —Going down a small hill, you find yourself in front of a vault to which some twenty steps lead down, where the clearest water gushes forth from the marble rocks. The enclosing little wall above, the tall trees which give shade all about, the coolness —all this makes the place so attractive and thrilling. Hardly a day passes without my sitting there for an hour. Then the girls will come from the town and fetch water, the most innocent task and the most necessary, in ancient times performed even by the daughters of kings. As I sit there, the patriarchal idea comes to life again for me: I see them, our forefathers, meet at the fountain and do their wooing, and feel how benevolent spirits hover around wells and springs. Anyone who has refreshed himself at a cool fountain after a long walk in summer will understand my feelings.

May 13

You ask me if you should send me my books? —My dear fellow, I implore you, for God's sake, do not bother me with them. No longer do I wish to be guided, excited, stimulated; my own heart storms enough in itself. What I need are cradlesongs, and I have found plenty of these in my Homer. How often do I lull my rebellious blood to rest, for you cannot imagine anything so erratic, so restless as my heart. My friend, need I tell you all this, you, whom I have so often burdened with the sight of my transitions from grief to excessive joy, from sweet melancholy to fatal passion. I treat my poor heart, moreover, as though it were a sick child, and satisfy all its desires. Do not tell this to anyone; there are those who would strongly disapprove.

May 15

The simple folk here already know me and have taken to me, especially the children. When I first joined them, and asked them in a friendly way about this or that, some thought that I wanted to scoff at them, and they sometimes even curtly rebuked me. I did not resent this; I merely felt most vividly what I had observed frequently before: people of a certain rank will always keep a cool distance from common people, as if they were afraid to lose their dignity by too much familiarity. On the other hand, there are superficial fellows and malicious jokers who seem to be condescending and only hurt the feelings of the poor folk all the more by their insolence. I know quite well that we are not and cannot ever be equal; but I am convinced that anyone who thinks it necessary to keep his distance from the so-called mob in order to gain its respect is as much to blame as the coward who hides from his enemy because he fears to be defeated.

A little while ago I came to the fountain and saw a young servant girl who had set her pitcher on the lowest step while she looked about for one of her companions to help her lift it to her head. I went down and looked at her. "Do you want me to help you?" I asked. She blushed all over. "Oh, no, sir!" she said. —"Why not?" —She adjusted the pad on her head, and I helped her. She thanked me and went up the steps.

May 17

I have made all sorts of acquaintances but have not yet found any congenial company. I do not know what there is about me that attracts people; so many like me and become attached to me, and then I am always sorry that we can travel only a short way together. When you ask me what the people here are like, I must answer: Like people everywhere! There is a certain monotony about mankind. Most people toil during the greater part of their lives in order to live, and the slender span of free time that remains worries them so much that they try by every means to get rid of it. O Destiny of Man!

They are a very good sort of people, however. Whenever I forget myself and enjoy in their company the pleasures still granted to human beings, can exchange friendly jokes in all frankness and candor around a well-set table, arrange a drive in a carriage or a ball at the proper time—all this sort of thing has quite a good effect on me; I must only avoid remembering that there are still many other forces dormant in me, all unused and rotting, which I must carefully hide. Ah!

it contracts my heart, and yet—it is the fate of a man like myself to be misunderstood.

Alas, that the friend of my youth is gone! Alas, that I ever knew her! I should say to myself: You are a fool to search for something that cannot be found on this earth. But she was mine, I felt her heart, her great soul, in whose presence I seemed to be more than I really was because I was all that I could be. Good God, was there a single force in my soul then unused? Could I not unfold in her presence all the wonderful emotions with which my heart embraces Nature? Was not our relationship a perpetual interweaving of the most subtle feeling with the keenest wit, whose modifications, however extravagant, all bore the mark of genius? And now?—Alas, the years she had lived in advance of my own brought her to the grave before me. I shall never forget her—neither her unwavering mind nor her divine fortitude.

A few days ago I met a young man by the name of V., an open-hearted youth with pleasant features. He has just left the university and does not consider himself a sage but thinks, nevertheless, that he knows more than other people. He has studied hard, as I can tell from many indications; in short, he has a pretty store of knowledge. As he had heard that I sketch a good deal and know Greek (two unusual phenomena in these parts), he came to see me and displayed all sorts of learning, from Batteux to Wood, from De Piles to Winckelmann, assuring me that he had read the whole first part of Sulzer's "Theory," and that he possessed a manuscript of Heyne's on the study of antiquity. I let that pass.

I have made the acquaintance of another good man, the Prince's bailiff, an honest, candid character. They say it warms the heart to see him among his children, of whom he has nine. There is much talk about his oldest daughter in particular. He invited me to his house, and I am going to pay him a visit soon. He lives an hour and a half from here in one of the Prince's hunting lodges which he was permitted to occupy after the death of his wife, as he found life here in town, and in his bailiff's quarters, too painful.

I have also come across a couple of odd people whom I consider thoroughly repulsive, and quite intolerable in their demonstrations of friendship.

Farewell! You will approve of this letter, which is entirely historical.

May 22

That the life of man is but a dream is a thought which has occurred to many people, and I myself am constantly haunted by it. When I see the limitations which imprison the active and speculative faculties of man; when I see how all human activity is directed toward procuring satisfaction for needs that have no other purpose than prolonging our miserable existence; when I see, moreover, how any comfort we may derive from certain points of inquiry is merely a dream-like kind of resignation, in which we paint our prison walls with gaily colored figures and luminous prospects—all this, Wilhelm, leaves me speechless. I withdraw into my inner self and there discover a world—a world, it is true, rather of vague perceptions and dim desires than of creative power and vital force. And then everything swims before my senses, and I go on smiling at the outer world like someone in a dream.

That children do not know the reason of their desires, all the learned teachers and instructors agree. But that grown-ups too stumble like children on this earth, not knowing whence they come or whither they go, acting as little according to true purposes, being ruled like them by cakes and birch rods, no one likes to believe; yet to me it seems quite obvious.

I know your reply to this statement, and I willingly admit that those are the happiest people who, like children, live for the day only, drag around their dolls, putting their clothes on or off, tiptoe around the cupboard where Mummy keeps the sweets locked up, and, after having finally snatched the desired bit, stand with full cheeks and shout: "More!" — These are indeed happy creatures. Nor are those people un-happy who, giving pompous names to their shabby occupa-tions or even to their passions, pretend that these are gigantic achievements for the happiness and welfare of mankind. Happy the man who can be like this! But whoever realizes in all humility what all this amounts to, who observes with what pleasure every prosperous citizen trims his little garden into a paradise, how patiently even the unfortunate man struggles along his road under the weight of his burden, and how all are eager to see the light of the sun a little longer— well, such a man remains calm and shapes his own world out of himself; and he, too, is happy because he is a human being. And then, however confined he may be, he still holds forever in his heart the sweet feeling of freedom, and knows that he can leave this prison whenever he likes.

May 26

You know of old my habit of settling down in some pleasant region and living there in a modest way. Here, too, I have discovered again a place which has attracted me.

About an hour from the town is a village called Wahlheim. Its location against a hill is very interesting, and when you leave it by the upper footpath, you can suddenly overlook the whole valley. The good landlady of the inn, pleasant and brisk for her age, provides beer, wine and coffee; and the best feature of all is two linden trees, shading with their spreading branches the little square in front of the church, which is framed on all sides by peasants' cottages, barns and farmyards. I have seldom found a place so intimate and charming, and often have my little table and a chair brought out from the inn, and there drink my coffee and read my Homer. When I came for the first time, quite by accident, on a fine afternoon, under these linden trees, I found the little square deserted. Everyone was out in the fields. Only one little boy, about four years of age, was sitting on the ground, holding another child of about six months, who sat between his feet close against his breast, so that his arms formed a kind of chair for the little one; and the older boy sat perfectly still in spite of the sprightly way in which he glanced around with his dark eyes. I was amused by the sight and, sitting down on a plow opposite the two, made a drawing of the brotherly pose with great delight. I included the nearest fence, a barn door, and a few broken cartwheels, just as they came into view, and realized, after an hour, that I had made a well-composed and very interesting sketch, without having added the slightest invention of my own. This confirmed me in my resolution to keep close to Nature in the future. Nature alone is illimitably rich, and Nature alone forms the great artist. It is possible to say a good deal in favor of rules, about as much as can be said in praise of bourgeois society. The person who takes his direction from rules alone will never produce anything in bad taste, in the same way as the person who allows himself to be shaped by rules of social convention can never become an intolerable neighbor or a conspicuous villain; on the other hand, any rule is likely to destroy both the true feeling of Nature and its true expression, whatever people may say to the contrary. You will object that this statement is too severe, and that rules only restrain and prune the overluxuriant vine, etc. My dear friend! Shall I give you an analogy? It is the same with love. A young man's heart is entirely attached to a girl; he spends every hour of the day with her, wastes all his strength, all his fortune, in order to prove to her at every moment that he is wholly devoted to her. Should a philistine then enter the picture, a man of some responsible position, and say to him: "My dear young man, it is natural to love, but you must love only in a sensible way. Organize your day; some hours for work and some—the hours of relaxation—for your sweetheart. Calculate your means; and it is perfectly permissible to use whatever is left over and beyond your personal needs to buy her a present of some sort, only not too frequently— perhaps for her birthday or a similar occasion." —Should the young man follow this advice, he will certainly turn into a useful member of society, and I should advise any prince to take him into his Cabinet; but his love is done with, and, if he is an artist, his art as well. O my friends! Why does the stream of genius so seldom break out as a torrent, with roaring high waves, and shake your awed soul? —Dear friends, because there are cool and composed gentlemen living on both banks, whose garden houses, tulip beds and cabbage fields would be devastated if they had not in good time known how to meet the threatening danger by building dams and ditches.

I am indulging, I see, in rapture, analogies and rhetoric, and I have forgotten to tell you the end of my story about the children. I had been sitting on my plow for almost two hours, completely absorbed in a painter's kind of perception which I described to you very fragmentarily in my letter of yesterday, when, toward evening, a young woman came up to the children, who had sat motionless the whole time. She carried a little basket on her arm and called from a distance: "Philip, you are a very good boy." She greeted me; I thanked her and, getting up, asked her if she was the children's mother. She said, yes, she was; and, handing a piece of bread to the older boy, she lifted the younger child on her arm and kissed it with motherly affection. "I asked Philip to take care of the little one," she said, "as I had to go to town with my oldest son to buy white bread, sugar, and an earthen pot." I noticed all these articles in her basket as the lid had fallen open. "I wanted to make some soup for Hans (that was the name of the youngest child), but his oldest brother, the rascal, had broken the old pot yesterday while he was quarreling with Philip for the scrapings." I asked about the oldest boy, and she had hardly mentioned the fact that he was chasing the geese in the meadow when he came running up with a hazel switch for his younger brother. I continued my talk with the woman and learned that she was the schoolmaster's daughter, and that her husband had gone to Switzerland to collect his inheritance from a cousin. "They meant to cheat him out of it," she said, "and did not answer his letters. That is why he went there himself. If only nothing has happened to him; I have not heard anything from him since he left." I was quite sorry to have to leave the woman, but I gave a penny to each boy, and another to the mother to buy a roll for the younger one whenever she went to town; and in this way we parted.

I tell you, my dearest friend, when I am completely beside myself, the tumult of my emotions is soothed by the sight of such a woman, who is rounding the narrow circle of her existence with serene cheerfulness, managing to make both ends meet from one day to the next, seeing the leaves fall without any thought save that winter is near.

Since then, I have often gone back there. The children are quite accustomed to me; they get sugar when I drink my coffee, and share my bread and butter and my curdled milk in the evening. On Sundays they never lack their penny, and, should I not be there after church, I have asked the landlady to give it to them.

They are quite familiar with me and tell me all sorts of things. I am particularly delighted to watch their show of temper and their naïve outbursts of greed whenever other children from the village are with them.

I took great pains to convince their mother not to worry that they might "bother the gentleman."

What I wrote you the other day about painting is certainly also true of poetry; one has only to recognize what is excellent and then have the courage to express it, which is, of course, easier said than done. Today I have come upon a little drama which, if truthfully written down, would make the loveliest idyll in the world; but why talk of poetry, drama, and idyll? Do we always have to dabble in literature when we are allowed to witness some natural happening?

If you should expect something noble and distinguished after this preamble, you will again be greatly disappointed. It was only a country lad who strongly attracted my sympathy. As usual, I shall be a bad narrator, and as usual, you will think my story is exaggerated. It is again Wahlheim and always Wahlheim that offers these exceptional characters and incidents.

I had been invited to drink coffee under the linden trees. As the people were not quite to my liking, I had found some pretext for not joining the party.

A young peasant came out of a nearby house and was soon busy mending the plow which I had sketched some days before. As I liked his manner, I spoke to him about his circumstances; we were soon acquainted and, as usually happens to me with such people, were soon quite familiar. He told me that he was in the service of a widow who treated him very well. He told me so much about her and praised her in such a way that I could soon guess that he was heart and soul devoted to her. She was no longer young, he said; her first husband had treated her badly, and she did not want to marry again. It became more than evident from his words how beautiful and how charming she was in his eyes, and how much he wished that she would choose him as a husband so that he might efface the memory of her first husband's faults. I should have to repeat every word of his story in order to give you a true picture of the pure affection, love, and devotion of this man. Yes, I should have to possess the gift of the greatest of poets in order to depict to you convincingly the expressiveness of his gestures, the harmony of his voice, the hidden fire of his eyes. No, words fail to convey the tenderness of his whole being; everything I could attempt to say about this would only be clumsy. I was particularly moved by his anxiety that I might receive a wrong impression about his relationship to her or doubt her respectability. The delightful way in which he spoke of her figure, her physical charm, that irresistibly attracted and captivated him in spite of her lack of real youth, I can only repeat to myself in my inmost soul. Never in my life have I seen an urgent and passionate desire combined with such purity of heart; yes, I may well say, never had I myself imagined or dreamed of such purity. Do not scold me if I confess that the memory of this innocence and candor fills my soul with delight, that the picture of this devotion and tenderness follows me everywhere, and that I thirst and languish as if kindled by that flame.

I shall try to see her as soon as possible, or rather, after giving it a second thought, I shall avoid her. It is better that I see her through the eyes of her lover; she might not appear to my own eyes, in reality, as I now see her; and why should I destroy the lovely image I already possess?

June 16

Why do I not write to you? And you, a learned man, ask me this? You should be clever enough to guess that I am in a happy mood because—in a word—I have made an acquaintance who moves my heart in a strange way. I have—I do not know.

It is not easy for me to tell you, in chronological order, just how it happened, how I met such a lovely being. I am contented and happy, and therefore not a good historian.

An angel! —Nonsense! Everyone calls his loved one thus, does he not? And yet I cannot describe to you how perfect she is, or why she is so perfect; enough to say that she has captured me completely.

So much innocence combined with so much intelligence; such kindness with such firmness; such inner serenity in such an active life.

But all this is foolish talk—pure abstract words which fail to describe one single feature of her real person. Another time—no, not another time, right at this moment I will tell you everything. If I don't do it now, it will never be done. Because—between you and me—since I began this letter I have been three times on the point of laying down my pen, having my horse saddled and riding out to her. Although I swore to myself this morning not to do it, I am going every other moment to the window to see how high the sun has climbed.

I could not bear it any longer; I had to see her. Here I am back, Wilhelm; I will now eat my supper and then go on writing to you. What a delight it was to see her among the dear lively children, her eight brothers and sisters!

But if I go on in this way you will know as little at the end as at the beginning. Listen, then, while I force myself to go into details.

The other day I wrote you that I had met the bailiff S., and that he had asked me to visit him in his hermitage, or rather, his little kingdom. I neglected to do so, and probably never would have gone there if I had not by chance discovered the treasure hidden in that quiet part of the district.

The young people here had arranged a ball in the country, and I gladly agreed to go. I asked a good, pretty, but otherwise uninteresting girl to be my partner, and proposed to hire a coach to drive out to the appointed place with her cousin and herself, picking up Charlotte S. on our way. "You will meet a beautiful girl," my partner said while we were driving through a broad clearing of the forest toward the hunting lodge. "Be careful that you do not fall in love with her!" her cousin added. —"What do you mean?" I said. —

"She is already engaged," was her answer, "and to a very worthy man who is not here at present. He left to attend to his affairs after the death of his father, and is also about to apply for an important position." This information did not particularly impress me.

The sun was still a quarter of an hour from the top of the mountains when we drove up at the lodge gate. The air was very close, and the ladies expressed their concern about a thunderstorm which was evidently gathering around the horizon in small compact whitish-gray clouds. I dispelled their fear by pretending to be a weather expert, although I myself began to feel apprehensive about an interruption of our amusement.

I climbed out of the coach, and the maid who came to the gate asked us to wait a moment—Mamsell Lottchen would soon be down. I crossed the courtyard toward the well-built lodge. When I had gone up the outer staircase and entered the house, I saw the most charming scene I had ever in my life beheld. In the entrance hall six children, between the ages of eleven and two, were swarming around a handsome young girl of medium height, who wore a simple white dress with pink bows on her arms and breast. She was holding a loaf of dark bread and cutting one slice apiece for each of the children around her, in proportion to age and appetite, dealing it out so kindly, and each child cried out "Thank you!" so artlessly, after having stretched out two tiny hands as high as possible before the slice was cut; after which they all cheerfully jumped away with their supper, or, if of a quieter nature, walked sedately toward the gate to have a look at the strangers and at the coach in which their Lotte would soon drive away. —"Please, forgive me," she said, "that I gave you the trouble to come for me, and that I keep the ladies waiting. While I was dressing and making all sorts of arrangements for the household during my absence, I forgot to give the children their supper, and they won't have their bread sliced by anyone but me." I paid her an insignificant compliment while my soul was taking in her whole appearance, her voice, the grace of her bearing; and I had just enough time to recover from my surprise when she ran to her room to fetch her gloves and fan. The children meanwhile kept at some distance, casting sidelong glances at me, and I went up to the youngest, an extremely pretty little boy. He drew back just as Lotte returned from her room, saying: "Louis, shake hands with your uncle." The boy obeyed her most trustingly, and I could not refrain from kissing him with affection, in spite of his runny little nose. "Uncle?" I asked, taking her hand. "Do you consider me worthy of being related to you?" —"Oh," she said with a merry smile, "our circle of relatives is very wide, and I should be sorry if you were to be the worst among them." —On leaving, she told Sophy, the next oldest to herself, a girl of about eleven, to take good care of the younger children, and to give her love to their father when he returned from his ride. She told the children to obey Sophy as they would herself, and some of them promised to do so; but a pert little blonde of some six years said: "But she is not you, dear Lotte. We love you much more." —The two older boys had climbed up behind the coach and, on my pleading for them, were allowed to accompany us to the edge of the wood if they promised not to fight with each other and to hold on fast.

Hardly had we taken our seats and the ladies exchanged their welcomes and their remarks on one another's dresses and particularly on one another's hats, and had gossiped a good deal about the people they expected to meet, when Lotte asked the coachman to stop and ordered her brothers to climb down. They insisted on kissing her hand once more, and the older one did so with all the tenderness which can be characteristic of a boy of fifteen, the younger one in a rough and boisterous way. Once more she sent her love to the younger children, and then we continued our drive.

The cousin asked if Lotte had finished the book she had recently sent her. "No, I have not," Lotte said; "I do not like it; you may have it back. And the one before it was not any better." I was amazed when, on my asking her what books she meant, she gave me the titles. I was struck by the show of character in everything she said; every word revealed fresh attractions, and her flashes of intelligence showed in her face, which seemed gradually to light up with pleasure when she felt that I understood her.

"When I was younger," she continued, "I liked nothing so much as novels. God knows how happy I was if I could sit in a corner on Sundays and share with heart and soul the fortunes and misfortunes of some Miss Jenny. And I won't deny that this sort of book still has some attraction for me; but, as

I have so little time now for reading, whatever I read has to be to my taste. And the author whom I like most of all is the one who takes me into my own world, where everything happens as it does around me, and whose story, nevertheless, becomes to me as interesting and as touching as my life at home, which is certainly not a paradise but is, on the whole, a source of inexpressible happiness to me."

I tried to hide my emotions at these words. I did not, it is true, succeed very well; for when I heard her speak casually, but with much truth, about *The Vicar of Wakefield* and about ———, I lost all my reserve and told her everything I wished to tell, and only noticed, after some time, when Lotte directed the conversation to the other two, that they had been sitting all the while with wide-open eyes, as if they were not there at all. Now and then the cousin puckered up her little nose mockingly, to which, however, I paid no attention.

The conversation turned to the pleasures of dancing. "If this passion should be a weakness," Lotte said, "I readily confess that I don't know anything to surpass dancing. And whenever I have something on my mind, I start strumming some *contredanse* on my clavichord (which is always out of tune), and then all is well."

How delighted I was to look into her dark eyes while she spoke. How my whole soul was fascinated by her warm lips and her glowing cheeks! I was so deeply lost in the excellence of her conversation that I often did not catch the very words by which she expressed her meaning! —All this you can imagine, as you know me well.

I climbed out of the coach as if in a dream when we stopped in front of the house where the ball would take place, and was so lost in my dreams, with the twilit world all about me, that I hardly noticed the music which rang out to us from the illuminated ballroom above.

Two gentlemen, Herr Audran and another whose name escapes me—who can remember all those names!—who were the partners of Lotte and her cousin, welcomed us at the coach door and took charge of their ladies, and I escorted my partner upstairs.

We went through the steps of a few minuets; I asked one lady after another for a dance, but it seemed that only the most disagreeable ones could not decide to end the dance with a clasp of the hand. Lotte and her partner started an *anglaise,* and you can imagine how delighted I was when she was in the same line with us from the beginning of the first figure. You should see her dance! She concentrates so completely—heart and soul—on the dance itself; her whole body is in harmony, as carefree and as ingenuous as if nothing else mattered, as if she had no other thoughts or feelings; and I am certain that at those moments everything else vanishes from her sight.

I asked her for the second *contredanse;* she promised me the third and assured me with the most charming frankness that she was very fond of dancing in the German way. "It is a custom here," she continued, "that any couple belonging together remain together for the German dance; but my partner is awkward at waltzing and will be grateful if I spare him the effort. Your lady cannot waltz either and does not like to; but I noticed during the *anglaise* that you waltz well; if you, therefore, want to be my partner in the German dance, do go and ask my partner for the favor, and I shall do the same with your lady." I accepted the promise by taking her hand, and we agreed that her partner should meanwhile entertain mine.

Now the dance began, and we enjoyed ourselves for some time, interlacing our arms in various ways. With what nimble grace she moved! And when at last we changed to waltzing, and all the couples revolved around one another like celestial bodies, there was at first, owing to the inefficiency of most of the dancers, a kind of mix-up. We were wise, and let the others have their fling, but as soon as the clumsiest had left the floor, we stepped out and held the ground firmly with another couple, Audran and his partner. Never have I danced so well! I was no longer a mortal being. To hold that loveliest creature in my arms and to whirl with her like the wind so that the surroundings disappeared—truly, Wilhelm, I swore to myself that a girl whom I loved, on whom I might have claims, should never be allowed to waltz with another man save myself, even if it would spell ruin for me. You will understand!

We took a few turns around the ballroom between dances, to recover our breath. Then she sat down, and the oranges I had secured for her, now the only ones left, had a good effect, except that whenever she shared a little slice in a dutiful way with a greedy lady sitting next to her, I was cut to the heart.

We were the second couple in the third *anglaise*. As we crossed and recrossed the lines of dancers and while I, God knows with what delight, clung to her arm and held her glance, which was reflecting the frankest and purest happiness, we met a lady who had caught my attention before, because of the amiable expression of a face not exactly young. She looked at Lotte with a smile, lifted a warning finger, and, whirling past, pronounced the name *Albert* twice with much emphasis.

"Who is Albert?" I asked Lotte, "if I am not too bold to ask." She was about to answer when we were forced to separate, so as to participate in the Great Figure Eight. I seemed to notice a thoughtful shadow on her brow as we kept passing each other. "Why should I keep it a secret from you?" she said, offering me her hand for the promenade. "Albert is a fine man to whom I am as good as engaged." This was, of course, no news to me (the ladies having spoken to me of the matter in the coach), and yet it was now in some way new to me, as I had never actually thought of it in relation to her, who had become so dear to me in so short a time. At any rate I entangled myself in the dance, became absent-minded and stumbled in between the wrong couple, so that everything was at sixes and sevens, and Lotte's presence of mind as well as much pushing and pulling were necessary quickly to restore order.

The dance was not yet finished when the lightning, for some time seen in flashes on the horizon and which I had always explained away as mere summer lightning, became more powerful, and the thunder drowned out the music. Three ladies ran out of the ranks of dancers, and their partners followed suit. Confusion became general and the music stopped. It is natural, when an accident or something terrifying surprises us in the midst of our pleasures, for us to be more impressed than usual, partly because of the so vividly felt contrast, and partly, even more, because our senses are then susceptible and therefore react much more strongly. To these causes I must attribute the strange grimaces that I noticed on the faces of several ladies. The wisest one sat down in a corner, with her back turned to the window, and covered her ears with her hands. A second one knelt in front of her, hiding her head in the lap of the other. A third pushed herself in between and, bathed in tears, hugged her sisters. Some wanted to drive home; others, even more at a loss, did not have enough presence of mind to check the advances of some *gourmets* who were busy capturing from the lips of the pretty ladies in distress their anxious prayers destined for Heaven. Some of the gentlemen had gone downstairs to smoke a quiet pipe; and the rest of the company did not refuse when the hostess had the sensible idea of showing them into a room protected by shutters and curtains. Hardly had they got there when Lotte began to arrange the chairs in a circle, inviting everyone to sit down and join in a parlor game.

I saw more than one fellow purse his lips and stretch himself in expectation of a delicious forfeit. "We are going to play 'Counting,'" Lotte said. "Attention now! I'll go round the circle from right to left, and you all must count in that way round and round, each of you the number that falls to him; but it must go like wildfire, and the person who hesitates or makes a mistake gets his (or her) ears boxed, and so on to a thousand." Well, it was great fun to watch her. She went around the circle with her arm outstretched. "One" counted the first; his neighbor "two"; "three" the next, and so on. Then Lotte began to go faster, faster, and faster, until someone made a mistake—bang! a slap on his ear, and while the others laughed the next also—bang! and faster and faster! I myself received two slaps and, greatly pleased, thought that they were harder than those she gave to others. General confusion and outbursts of laughter brought the game to an end before the "thousand" had been counted. Groups of friends disappeared into the background; the thunderstorm was over, and I followed Lotte into the ballroom. On the way there she said: "They forgot the thunderstorm and everything else while they played the game." I did not know what to say. "I was one of the most frightened," Lotte continued, "but by playing the brave one, in order to cheer up the others, I became courageous myself."

We stepped to the window. The thunder could still be heard in the distance, and the blessed rain fell gently on the ground, from which the most refreshing fragrance rose to us on the fullness of the warm air. She stood leaning on her elbow, her eyes searching the landscape; she looked up at the sky and then at me. I saw her eyes fill with tears; she laid her hand on mine and said: "Klopstock!" I remembered immediately the magnificent ode which she had in mind, and was overcome by the flood of emotions which she evoked in me with this name. It was more than I could bear. I bowed over her hand and kissed it, moved to the happiest tears. And I again looked into her eyes—noble poet! if you had seen the deep reverence in her eyes! May I never hear again from other lips your so often profaned name!

June 19

I have forgotten where I stopped in my story the other day. I only know that it was two o'clock in the morning when I went to bed, and that if I could have chatted with you instead of writing to you, I should probably have kept you awake until daybreak.

I have not yet told you what happened when we drove home from the ball, and I have not the time to tell you today.

It was a magnificent sunrise. The dripping forest and the refreshed fields lay all about us! Our companions were dozing. Lotte asked me if I would not like to do the same; I should not take any notice of her. "So long as I see these eyes open," I said, looking into hers intensely, "there is no danger of my falling asleep." And we both kept awake until we arrived at her gate, which was noiselessly opened by the maid, who assured Lotte that her father and the children were well and still asleep. Then I left her, after asking the favor of seeing her again that same day. She granted my request and I went. Since then, sun, moon, and stars may continue on their course; for me there is neither day nor night, and the entire universe about me has ceased to exist.

June 21

My days are as blissful as those which God reserves for his saints; and, whatever may happen to me, I shall never be able to say that I have not experienced the purest joys of life. —You know my Wahlheim. I am now completely settled here. It is only half an hour to Lotte's home, where I feel like myself and find all the happiness granted to man.

Had I known, in choosing Wahlheim as the goal of my walks, that it lies so near to Heaven! How often, in my wanderings near and far, have I seen the hunting lodge which now encloses all my desires, sometimes from the mountain, at other times across the river from the plain!

Dear Wilhelm, I have thought over many things concerning man's ambition to extend himself, to make new discoveries, to roam about; and, on the other hand, his inner urge voluntarily to submit to limitation, to jog along in the groove of habit without looking to right or left. It is strange how, when I came here and looked down from the mountain into the lovely valley, everything attracted me. There was the grove! Ah, could I but mingle with its shades! There was the mountaintop! Ah, could I but overlook from there the wide landscape! The interlocked hills and familiar valleys! Ah, could I but lose myself in them! —I hurried here and there and came back, not having found what I hoped to find. Oh, it is the same with the distance as with the future! A vast, twilit whole lies before our soul; our emotions lose themselves in it as do our eyes, and we long to surrender our entire being and let ourselves sink into one great well of blissful feeling. Alas, when we approach, when There has become Here, everything is as it was before, and we are left with our poverty, our narrowness, while our soul thirsts for comfort that slipped away.

So the most restless vagabond yearns in the end for his native land, and finds in his poor hut, in the arms of his wife, in the circle of his children, and in his labor to support them all, the happiness he searched the wide world for in vain.

When I walk in the morning at sunrise to my Wahlheim and pick my own dish of green peas in the garden of the inn, sit down and shell them while I read my Homer, and then choose a pan in the kitchen, cut off some butter and put the peas on the fire, covering the pan and sitting down so that I may shake them from time—I feel vividly how the wanton suitors of Penelope slaughtered oxen and swine, cut them up, and roasted them. There is nothing that fills me with more quiet, genuine emotion than those features of patriarchal life which I can, thank God, weave without affectation into my own way of living. How happy I am that my heart is open to the simple, innocent delight of the man who brings a head of cabbage to his table which he himself has grown, enjoying not only the cabbage but all the fine days, the lovely mornings when he planted it, the pleasant evenings when he watered it, so that, after having experienced pleasure in its growth he may, at the end, again enjoy in one single moment all that has gone before.

June 29

The day before yesterday the physician came out here to see the bailiff and found me on the floor among Lotte's children, as some crawled over me, and others teased me, while my tickling them brought on loud cries. The doctor, very dogmatic and stiff as a puppet, who arranges the pleats of his cuffs and pulls out the endless frills of his jabot as he talks, thought all this to be beneath the dignity of an intelligent person, as I saw from the way he turned up his nose. I did not let him discourage me, however; and, while he was discussing very rational matters, I rebuilt the houses of cards that the children had knocked down. He later went all over town complaining that the bailiff's children were naughty enough but that Werther would now spoil them completely.

Yes, dear Wilhelm, children are nearer my heart than anything else on earth. When I watch them and see in these little creatures the seeds of all the virtues, all the forces they will need one day so badly; when I see in their obstinacy the future perseverance and firmness of character, in their mischievousness the happy temper and the facility needed to evade the world's dangers, all so natural and innocent!—always, always I keep repeating the golden words of the Teacher of mankind: Unless ye become even as one of these! And yet, dearest friend, we treat them, who are our equals, whom we should look upon as our models, as our subjects. We don't want them to have a will of their own! —Do *we* not have one? And in what lies our privilege? Because we are older and wiser! —Good Lord, from your Heaven you look down on nothing but old children and young children; and your Son has already long ago proclaimed in which age you find greater joy. That people believe in Him and yet do not listen to His words—this also is an old story—and model their children upon themselves, and—farewell, Wilhelm! I do not wish to rave any longer.

July 1

What Lotte's presence must mean to a sick person I can feel in my own poor heart, which is worse off than many a one that pines on a sickbed. She is going to spend some days in the town with a good woman who, from what the doctors say, is nearing her end and wishes to have Lotte at her bedside in her last moments. A week ago I accompanied Lotte on her visit to the pastor of St. ——, a little village, about an hour away, in the mountains. We arrived there at about four in the afternoon. Lotte had brought her second sister with her. On entering the courtyard of the parsonage, shaded by two tall walnut trees, we found the good old man sitting on a bench in front of the house door; when he saw Lotte, he became very animated, forgot his knotty stick and tried to get up and meet her. She ran toward him, made him sit down again while she seated herself at his side, gave him her father's warmest greetings, and hugged his ugly, dirty youngest boy, the apple of his old father's eye. You should have seen her holding the old man's attention with her talk, raising her voice to reach his almost deaf ears; telling him about the healthy young people who had died unexpectedly, about the excellent effects of Karlsbad, and praising his resolution to go there next summer; and saying how she thought he looked much better and brisker than the last time she had seen him. Meanwhile, I was being polite to the pastor's wife. The old man became very cheerful. And as I could not help but admire the beautiful walnut trees that shaded us so pleasantly, he began to tell us, although with some difficulty, their history. "We don't know," he said, "who planted the older one; some say this pastor, others that one. But the younger tree, behind there, is as old as my wife, fifty next October. Her father planted it the morning of the day she was born. He was my predecessor here, and I cannot tell you how much he loved that tree, and certainly it is no less dear to me. My wife was sitting under it on a log with her knitting when I first entered this courtyard as a poor student twenty-seven years ago." Lotte inquired after his daughter and was told she had gone out to the laborers in the field with a Herr Schmidt, and the old man took up his story again: how his predecessor had grown fond of him, and his daughter as well; and how he had become first his curate and then his successor. He had hardly finished his story when his daughter came through the garden with Herr Schmidt. She welcomed Lotte with warm affection, and I confess that I found her very pleasing: a lively brunette with a shapely figure, who might have been an entertaining companion during a short stay in the country. Her suitor (for Herr Schmidt was obviously this) was an educated but reserved man who refused to join the conversation, although Lotte kept trying to draw him in. What most distressed me was that I gathered from the expression on his face that it was obstinacy and moodiness rather than limited intelligence that kept him from communication. This fact became gradually only too clear; for when Friederike, later on our walk, changed places with Lotte and, occasionally, with me, the gentleman's face, swarthy by nature, darkened so visibly that soon Lotte tugged my sleeve, giving me to understand that I had been too polite to Friederike. Now, nothing makes me more angry than people who torment one another, particularly if young people in the prime of their lives, when they should be most receptive of all pleasures, mutually spoil their few good days by putting on moody faces, realizing only when it is too late that they have wasted something irrecoverable. It greatly annoyed me; and when we had returned to the parsonage, toward evening, and were seated around the table drinking our milk, and the conversation turned toward the joys and sorrows of this world, I could not help but pick up the thread and fervently attack bad moods. "We human beings often complain," I began, "that there are so few good days and so many bad ones; but I think we are generally wrong. If our hearts were always open to enjoy the good, which God gives us every day, then we should also have enough strength to bear the evil, whenever it comes." —"But we cannot command our dispositions," said the pastor's wife. "How much depends on the body! If one does not feel well, everything seems wrong." —I admitted that. "Then," I said, "we'll look at moodiness as a disease and see if there is a remedy for it." —"That makes sense," said Lotte. "I, for one, believe at least that much depends on ourselves. I speak from my own experience. If something irritates me and is about to make me depressed, I jump up and sing a few dance tunes up and down the garden, and immediately the mood is gone." — "That is just what I wanted to say," I replied. "Bad humor is exactly like laziness, because it is a kind of laziness. Our nature has a strong inclination toward both, and yet, if we are strong enough to pull ourselves together, our work is quickly and easily done, and we find real pleasure in activity." Friederike listened very attentively, but her young man made the objection that man is not his own master, least of all master of his emotions. "Here we are speaking of an unpleasant emotion," I rejoined, "and certainly everyone would like to elude it. No one knows the extent of his powers unless he has tested them thoroughly. A sick person will certainly consult all available doctors and will not reject the greatest suffering or the bitterest medicine if he can recover the good health he longs for." I noticed that the good old pastor was straining his ears to catch the gist of our discussion, and I raised my voice and turned to him. "They preach against so many vices," I said, "but I never heard anyone attacking bad humor from the pulpit." "The pastors in towns should do just that," he said. "The peasants are never ill-humored; but a little preaching might do no harm here sometimes, and it would at least be a lesson for my wife and for the bailiff." Everyone laughed, and he heartily joined in, until he was seized by a fit of coughing that for a time interrupted our conversation. Then the young man began to speak once more: "You call bad humor a vice; I think that an exaggeration." —"Not at all," I retorted, "if that which harms oneself as well as one's neighbor deserves the name. Is it not enough that we cannot make each other happy; should we in addition deprive each other of that pleasure which every heart may sometimes grant itself? And give me the name of the man who is in a bad mood and yet gallant enough to hide it, to bear it alone without blighting other people's happiness! Or is it not perhaps an inner resentment at our own unworthiness, a dissatisfaction with ourselves, which is always bound up with some envy stirred up by foolish vanity?

We see people happy whom we have not made happy, and that is unbearable to us." Lotte gave me a smile, having noticed the emotion with which I spoke, and a tear in the eye of Friederike spurred me on to continue. —"Woe to them," I said, "who abuse their power over the hearts of others and deprive them of any simple joy which there has its source. All the gifts, all the favors in the world cannot for a moment replace the inner happiness which the envious moodiness of our tyrant has spoiled."

My whole heart was full at this moment; the memory of past events rushed into my mind, and my eyes filled with tears.

"If people would only warn themselves daily," I exclaimed, "that one cannot do anything for one's friends but leave them their pleasure and add to their happiness by sharing it with them. Are you able to give them one drop of comfort when their souls are tormented by a violent passion or crushed by grief?

"And when the last fatal sickness assails the beloved whom you have worn out in the days of her youth, and she lies prostrate in pitiable exhaustion, her unseeing eyes fixed on Heaven, the cold sweat of death coming and going on her pale forehead, and you stand at the bedside like a condemned man with the desperate feeling that you can do nothing; and you feel agony cramp your heart so that you wish to sacrifice all in order to inspire the dying person with one invigorating drop, one spark of courage . . ."

The memory of a similar scene at which I had been present completely overwhelmed me as I said these words. I raised my handkerchief to my eyes and left the company. Only the voice of Lotte, who called out to me that it was time to leave, brought me to myself. And how she scolded me on our way home for my too warm sympathy with everything, saying it would be my ruin and that I should spare myself! O angel, for your sake I must live!

July 6

She stays with her dying friend and is ever the same active, lovely creature whose presence soothes pain and makes people happy wherever she goes. She went for a walk last evening with Marianne and her youngest sister. I knew of it, and went to meet them, and we walked together. After an hour and a half we returned to the town and stopped at the fountain which is so dear to me, and now will be a thousand times dearer. Lotte sat down on the little wall above, and we stood near her. I looked around and alas! the time when my heart was so lonely returned vividly to my mind. —"Dear fountain," I said, "it is a long time since I rested near your coolness; I have sometimes even passed by in a hurry without giving you a glance." —I looked down and saw the little girl coming up the steps, carefully carrying a glass of water. I looked at Lotte and felt deeply what she means to me. Meanwhile, the child approached with the glass, and Marianne wanted to take it from her, but "No!" cried the little one with the sweetest expression. "No, you must drink first, Lotte!" I was so delighted with the candor, the goodness, with which these words were said, that I could not otherwise express my emotion but lifted the child in my arms and kissed her so fervently that she immediately began to scream and to weep. "That was not right of you," said Lotte. —I was puzzled. —"Come, darling," she continued, taking the child by the hand and leading her down the steps. "There, wash your face, quick, quick, in the clear spring water, and everything will be all right again." —While I stood watching the little girl rub her cheeks with her wet little hands, so trustful that the miraculous spring water would wash away the defilement, and remove the chance of being disgraced by an ugly beard; and when I heard Lotte say: "Now, that will do!" (but the child went on washing herself eagerly, as though Much would help more than Little)—I tell you, Wilhelm, never did I attend a ceremony of baptism with more reverence; and when Lotte came up the steps again, I would gladly have knelt before her, as before a prophet who has washed away with holy water the crimes of a nation.

That same evening, in the happiness of my heart, I could not help repeating the little incident to a man I thought to have common sense, as he is intelligent; but what was his reaction! He said that Lotte had been very thoughtless; that one should never deceive children; such deceit would give rise to innumerable misconceptions and superstitions from which children should be protected at an early age. —It came to my mind that there had been a christening in the man's family only a week ago; therefore I changed the subject but in my heart remained faithful to the truth: that we should deal with children as God deals with us; and He makes us happiest when He lets us stagger about under a benign delusion.

July 8

What children we are! How we crave for a noticing glance! We had gone to Wahlheim. The ladies were driving out, and during our walks together I thought I saw in Lotte's eyes— but I am a fool. Forgive me; you should see those eyes. I must be brief, for I am so sleepy that I can hardly keep my eyes open. —Well, the ladies were getting into the carriage and young W., Selstadt, Audran, and I were standing around it. There was a lively conversation going on through the carriage door with the other young men, who were lighthearted and talkative enough. I tried to catch Lotte's glance. Alas, it wandered from one young man to the other, but it did not fall on me! Me! Me! Who stood there absorbed in her alone! My heart bade her a thousand farewells, and she did not notice me! The carriage drove off, and tears stood in my eyes. I looked after her, and saw Lotte's headdress lean out of the carriage window as she turned to look back—ah, at me? Dear friend, I am torn by this uncertainty. My only consolation is:

She may have turned to look back at me! Perhaps! Good night! Oh, what a child I am!

You should see what an absurd figure I cut when people talk about her in company! Even more so if they ask me how I like her—like! I hate the word like poison. What sort of a person is he who likes Lotte, whose heart and mind is not completely possessed by her! Like! The other day someone asked me if I "liked" Ossian!

Frau M. is very ill indeed; I pray for her life because I suffer with Lotte. I rarely see her at my friend's, but today she told me a curious incident. Old M. is a hard, close-fisted man who has tormented and kept a tight rein on his wife all during her lifetime, but she has always succeeded in managing somehow. A few days ago, when the doctor had given up hope for her, she sent for her husband—Lotte was in the room—and said to him: "I have to confess something that might cause confusion and annoyance after my death. Until lately I have managed the household as neatly and as economically as possible; but you will forgive me for having deceived you during the last thirty years. At the beginning of our married life you fixed a very small sum for the purchase of food and for other domestic expenses. When our household became larger and our business grew, you could not be persuaded to raise my weekly allowance in proportion; you very well know that when our expenses were heaviest, you required me to manage on seven florins a week. I accepted this money without protest, but I took the balance needed from the weekly receipts, as nobody suspected that your wife would steal from your till. I have not squandered the money, and I might have met Eternity with hope and confidence, even without confessing all this, if I had not thought of the woman who will have to keep house after me, and who may be at a loss how to make ends meet, as you will always insist then that your first wife managed with so little."

I spoke to Lotte about the incredible delusion of a man who does not suspect that there must be something wrong when a person manages with seven guilders and expenses are obviously perhaps twice as much. But I have personally known people who would accept the presence of the prophet's "unfailing cruse of oil" in their home without being surprised.

No, I do not deceive myself! In her dark eyes I have read a genuine sympathy for me and my destiny. Yes, I feel—and in this I can trust my heart—that she—oh, may I, can I express the Heaven that exists in these words?—that she loves me!

Loves me!—And how precious I become in my own eyes, how I—to you as an understanding person I may say it—how I admire myself since she loves me.

Is this presumption, or a sense of true proportion? I do not know the man whom I once feared as a rival in Lotte's heart. And yet, when she speaks of her fiancé with such warmth, such affection, I feel like one who has been deprived of all his honors and titles and who has had to yield his sword.

Oh, how my blood rushes through my veins when my fingers unintentionally brush hers or when our feet touch under the table. I shrink back as though from fire, but a secret force drives me forward again, although everything swims before my eyes. Her innocent, candid soul does not divine how tormenting such small intimacies can be. And when, while we talk, she puts her hand on mine and, animated by what we are saying, moves closer to me, so that the heavenly breath of her mouth reaches my lips, I am close to fainting, as if struck by lightning. And, Wilhelm, if I should ever dare—this heavenly confidence—you understand! No, my heart is not so depraved! Weak! Weak enough!—And is that not depravity?

She is sacred to me. Any desire is silenced in her presence. I never know what I feel when I am with her; it is as if my soul were spinning through every nerve. She plays a melody on her clavichord with the touch of an angel, so simple, so ethereal! It is her favorite tune, and I am cured of all pain, confusion, and melancholy the moment she strikes the first note.

Not one word about the magic power of music in antiquity seems to me improbable when I am under the spell of her simple melody. And how well she knows when to play it, at the moment when I feel like blowing out my brains. The confusion and darkness of my soul are then dispersed, and I can breathe more freely again.

July 18

Wilhelm, what would the world mean to our hearts without love! What is a magic lantern without its lamp! As soon as you insert the little lamp, then the most colorful pictures are thrown on your white wall. And even though they are nothing but fleeting phantoms, they make us happy as we stand before them like little boys, delighted at the miraculous visions. I have not been able to see Lotte today; a party which I could not refuse to attend prevented me from going. What should I do? I sent my servant to her, only so that I might have someone near me who had been in her presence today. How impatiently I waited for his return, how happy I was to see him back. I should have liked to take him by his shoulder and kiss him, if I had not been too embarrassed to do so.

It is said that the Bologna stone, when placed in the sun, absorbs the sun's rays and is luminous for a while in the dark. I felt the same with the boy. The consciousness that her eyes had rested on his face, his cheeks, the buttons of his jacket and the collar of his overcoat, made all these sacred and precious to me. At that moment I would not have parted with him for a thousand taler. I felt so happy in his presence. God forbid that you should laugh at me, Wilhelm. Are these delusions if they make us so happy?

July 19

"I am going to see her," is my first cry in the morning when I rouse myself and gaze at the glorious sun in a perfectly serene mood. "I am going to see her!" And thus I have no other wish for the rest of the day. Everything, everything is drowned in this prospect.

July 20

I cannot yet accept your suggestion that I should accompany the envoy to——. I am not very fond of a subordinate position; and we all know that the man is a disgusting fellow, besides. You write that my mother would like to see me doing some active work; it makes me laugh. Am I not now active? and does it make any real difference whether I count peas or lentils? As everything in the world amounts after all to nothing to speak of, a person who drudges for the sake of others, for money or honors or what not, without following his own ambition, his own need, is always a fool.

July 24

Since you are so concerned that I should not neglect my drawing, I would rather skip that subject than confess that I have not done much lately.

Never before have I been happier, never has my sensitiveness to Nature been richer or deeper, even to the smallest stone, the tiniest blade of grass, and yet—I do not know how to express myself, but my powers of perception are so weak that everything floats and fluctuates before my mind, so that I cannot seize any outline; but I imagine I could do better if I had some clay or wax. I shall get some clay if this state lasts much longer, and I shall knead away even if cakes should be the outcome.

Three times I have started Lotte's portrait, and three times I have bungled it, which makes me very cross, the more so because I was at one time quite successful in getting likenesses. Finally I gave up and cut her silhouette, and with that I shall be satisfied.

July 26

Yes, dear Lotte. I shall order and look after everything; please keep on giving me commissions, and frequent ones. But I ask you one favor: no more sand in the notes you write me. I took today's quickly to my lips, and something gritted between my teeth.

July 26

Many times I have made up my mind not to see her so often. If one could only stick to one's resolutions! Every day I succumb to temptation, and then promise myself most solemnly that I shall stay away tomorrow for once; but when tomorrow comes, I again find some irresistible reason to go, and, before I know it, I am with her. Either she has said the night before, "You will come tomorrow, won't you?" and who could then stay away? Or she has given me some errand, and I think it is proper to bring her the answer in person; or the day is so very lovely that I walk to Wahlheim, and, when I am there, it is only half an hour to her! —I am so close to her aura—zut! and I am there. My grandmother knew a fairy tale about the Magnetic Mountain. Ships which sailed too close to it were suddenly deprived of all their iron; all the nails flew toward the mountain, and the poor sailors were shipwrecked among the collapsing planks.

July 30

Albert has arrived, and I shall go away. Even if he were the best, the most noble person, one to whom I would be willing to submit myself in every respect—it would still be unbearable to see him before my eyes in possession of so much perfection. Possession! —Enough, Wilhelm, the Bridegroom is here! A worthy, agreeable man whom one cannot help liking. Fortunately, I was not present when he was welcomed back. That would have torn my heart. He has so much sense of decorum that he has not once kissed Lotte in my presence. God bless him! I must love him for the respect with which he treats her. For me he has the kindest feelings, but I suspect that this is Lotte's doing rather than an impulse of his own spirit; for in these matters women have a delicate way, and they are right; if they can keep two devoted admirers on mutual good terms the advantage is always on their side, although it is rarely achieved.

Meanwhile I cannot deny Albert my esteem. His outward composure is in very strong contrast to the restlessness which I cannot conceal of my own character. He feels deeply, and he knows what he possesses in Lotte. He seems seldom to be in a bad mood, a sin which, as you know, I hate more in human beings than any other.

He thinks me a person of sensitive intelligence; and my devotion to Lotte, my warm enthusiasm for everything she does, increases his triumph, and he loves her all the more. I am undecided whether he may not sometimes torment her with petty jealousy; were I in his place, I would not be entirely free from that demon.

Be that as it may! My happiness with Lotte is gone. Shall I call this folly or delusion? What are names! The situation itself is evident. I knew everything I now know before Albert returned; I knew that I could not make any claims upon her, nor did I make any; so far, that is, as it is possible for one not to feel desire in the presence of such sweetness. And yet the idiot now stares with wide eyes because the other man really arrives and carries off the girl.

I firmly set my teeth and mock at my misery: and I would mock twice and thrice at anyone who might suggest that I should resign myself, since nothing can be helped in any case. Don't pester me with those empty-headed people! —I roam about in the woods, and when I arrive at Lotte's house and find Albert sitting with her in the arbor in her garden, and I cannot then leave, I behave in a wild and boisterous way and start all sorts of tomfooleries. "For Heaven's sake," said Lotte to me today, "please don't make a scene, as you did last night! You are dreadful when you show off in that way." Between ourselves, I wait for the time when Albert is busy; then zut! I am there; and I am always happy when I find her alone.

August 8

Please, dear Wilhelm, do not think that I had you in mind when I called those people intolerable who ask us to resign ourselves to an inevitable fate. I really never thought for a moment that you could hold such an opinion. And, fundamentally, you are right. I have only one objection: in this world we are seldom faced with an Either-Or; all emotions and modes of action show as many varieties of shape and shading as exist between a hooked nose and one that is turned up.

So you won't be angry with me when I grant your whole argument, and yet continue in my attempt to slip in between the Either and the Or.

"Either," you say, "you have some reason to hope, so far as Lotte is concerned, or you have none. Very well, in the first case, try to carry the matter through; try to reach the fulfillment of your wishes. Otherwise, pull yourself together and try to get rid of an unfortunate passion that is bound to burn up all your energy." My dear friend! That is well said, and easily said.

But can you demand it of the unhappy man whose whole life is slowly and irremediably wasting away of a lingering disease; can you demand that he should make a definite end of his misery by the stab of a dagger? And does not the disease, at the very same time that it burns up his strength, also destroy the courage he needs to free himself from it?

In the evening

My diary, which I have neglected for some time, fell into my hands today, and I am amazed how I ran into this situation with full awareness, step by step. How clearly I have seen my condition, yet how childishly I have acted. How clearly I still see it, and yet show no sign of improvement.

August 10

If I were not an idiot, I could lead the best and happiest of lives. One cannot easily imagine the union of pleasanter circumstances for anyone than that in which I am now placed.

Oh, how true it is that our heart alone creates its own happiness! To be a member of this charming family, to be loved by the father like a son, by the children like a father, and by Lotte! —And then there is that worthy Albert, who never disturbs my happiness by peevish bad manners; who meets me with warm friendship; for whom I am, next to Lotte, the most cherished being in the world. Wilhelm, it is a joy to hear us talk about Lotte on our walks together. There is nothing more ridiculous on this earth than our relationship; and yet I am often moved to tears when I think of it.

When he tells me of Lotte's kindly mother; how on her deathbed she entrusted Lotte with the care of her household and her children, and Lotte herself to Albert's care; how from that day on Lotte had been animated by an entirely new spirit; how she had conscientiously taken over the house and become a real mother to the children; how not one moment of her time had been spent without tasks and active love, and yet she kept her former cheerfulness and lightness of heart. —While he talks I walk along beside him and pick wayside flowers, arrange them carefully into a nosegay, and —throw them into the river which flows beside the path, and watch them float gently downstream. —I do not remember if I wrote you that Albert is going to remain here; he will receive a handsome salary from a position with the Court, where he is in great favor. I have seldom seen his equal in regard to order and diligence in handling affairs.

Albert is certainly the best man under the sun. Yesterday a remarkable scene took place between us. I went to take leave of him because I was suddenly seized by the desire to ride into the mountains, where I am now writing you. As I paced up and down his room I caught sight of a brace of pistols. "Will you lend me your pistols for my trip?" I asked him. "By all means," he replied, "if you will take the trouble to load them; I only keep them here *pro forma.*" I took one of them down, and he continued: "Since the day that my precaution paid me a nasty trick, I do not want to have anything more to do with that sort of thing." I was curious to hear the story. —"I was staying," he said, "for about three months with a friend in the country. I had taken along an unloaded pair of pistols, and I slept unconcerned. One rainy afternoon when I was sitting about, doing nothing, the thought crossed my mind—I do not know why—that we might be attacked and might need the pistols—you know how one sometimes imagines things. I gave them to the servant to clean and load. He was dallying with the maids and wanted to scare them, when, God knows how, the pistol went off. The ramrod was still in the barrel and struck the ball of the right thumb of one of the girls and smashed it. Of course, I had to pay for her tears as well as for the medical treatment; and since that day I have left all my firearms unloaded. But, dear friend, what is the use of caution? One never learns enough about danger! Although—" You already know that I am very fond of the fellow up to the point when he says "although." For does it not go without saying that any general statement has its exceptions? But he is so scrupulous that when he thinks he has said anything rash or commonplace or only partly true, he does not stop qualifying, modifying, adding and subtracting until, at last, there is nothing left of the subject. On this occasion he became so deeply entangled in the matter that I finally did not listen to him any longer. I suddenly became dejected, and, with a violent gesture, pressed the mouth of the pistol to my forehead above the right eye. "Come, come," Albert exclaimed, taking the pistol from me, "what are you doing?" —"It is not loaded," I said. —"Even so, what's the idea?" he retorted impatiently. "I cannot imagine how a person can be so foolish as to shoot himself; the mere thought of it is repulsive."

"Why must people like you," I exclaimed, "when you discuss any action, immediately say: 'This is foolish, that is wise; this is good, that is bad!' And what does it all mean? Does it mean that you have really discovered the inner circumstances of an action? Do you know how to explain definitely the reason why it happened, why it had to happen? If you indeed knew, you would be less hasty in your judgments."

"You will have to admit," said Albert, "that certain actions remain vicious, from whatever motives they may have risen."

I shrugged my shoulders and granted him that. "But, dear friend," I continued, "even in that general case, a few exceptions can exist. It is true that theft is a vice; but does the man who goes out to steal in order to save himself and his family from starvation—does he deserve pity or punishment? Who will be the first to cast a stone at the husband who sacrifices to his just indignation his unfaithful wife and her vile seducer? Or at the young girl who in one blissful hour loses herself in the irresistible joys of love? Even our laws themselves, those cold-blooded pedants, can be moved toward clemency, and refrain from punishing."

"It is quite a different matter," Albert replied, "when a man is carried away by his passions and loses all power of reflection; he can then be considered a drunkard or a madman."

"O you rational people," I exclaimed, smiling. "Passion! Drunkenness! Madness! You stand there so complacently, without any real sympathy, you moralists, condemning the drunkard, detesting the madman, passing by like the Levite, and thanking God that you are not made as one of these. I myself have been drunk more than once; my passions have never been very far removed from madness, and yet I do not feel any remorse. For I have learned in my own way that all unusual people who have accomplished something great or seemingly impossible have always been proclaimed to be drunk or mad.

"But even in everyday life it is unbearable to hear people say of almost anyone who acts in a rather free, noble or unexpected way: 'That man is drunk, or he is crazy!' Shame on you sober ones! Shame on you sages!"

"Now, that is another of your whims," said Albert. "You exaggerate everything, and you are certainly wrong when you compare suicide, which we discuss here, to great actions, since no one can consider it as anything but a weakness. For it is certainly easier to die than bravely to bear a life of misery."

I was about to break off, as no kind of argument upsets me more than when someone utters a trivial commonplace while I am speaking from the heart. But I kept my temper, because I had heard this sort of talk only too often and had been annoyed by it many times before. Therefore I replied rather forcibly: "You call that weakness? Please, don't be misled by appearances. Would you call a nation weak that groans under the intolerable yoke of a tyrant, when it at last rises and breaks its chains? A man, horrified that his house has caught fire, feels all his strength tighten and carries with ease burdens that he would scarcely be able to move in a calmer mood; or a man in the rage of having been insulted takes on single-handed half a dozen opponents and defeats them—can such people be called weak? If, my friend, exertion means strength, why should overexertion mean the opposite?" —Albert looked at me and said, "Don't be offended if I say that the examples you give me are irrelevant to our subject." —"That may be so," I replied. "People have often reproached me for my irrational way of associating things, a way which, they say, often verges on absurdity. Let us see if we have any other way of imagining how a person may feel when he has decided to throw off the ordinarily agreeable burden of life, for only insofar as we can enter into an-other's emotions have we the right to discuss such matters.

"Human nature," I continued, "has its limits; it can bear joy, suffering, and pain to a certain degree, but it collapses as soon as that degree is exceeded. The question, therefore, is not whether someone is weak or strong, but what degree of suffering he can actually endure, be it moral or physical; and I find it just as strange to call a man who takes his own life a coward as it would be improper to call a coward a man who is dying of a malignant fever."

"Paradoxical! Very paradoxical!" Albert exclaimed. — "Not so much as you may think," I replied. "You admit that we call a disease fatal which attacks Nature so violently that her forces are partly consumed or so largely put out of action that they cannot recover and restore the ordinary course of life by some lucky turn.

"Now, my friend, let us apply this same sort of reasoning to the mind. Let us watch man in his limited sphere and see how impressions affect him, how he is obsessed by ideas, until finally a growing passion robs him of any possible calmness of mind and becomes his ruin.

"A composed, sensible person who has a clear view of the condition of the unfortunate man tries in vain to give advice; just as the healthy man, standing at the bedside of the sick, is unable to transfer to the latter the smallest fraction of his own strength."

Albert thought all this too general in expression. I re-minded him of a girl who had been found in the river,

drowned some time before, and told him again her history.
—She was a good-natured young creature who had grown
up within a narrow circle of domestic tasks weekly laid out
for her, with no other prospect of possible amusement than
Sunday walks about town with her friends, dressed in her
Sunday finery which she had gradually acquired; or perhaps
once in a long while a dance; or an occasional lively chat
with a neighbor interested in the source of a quarrel, or
some slander—a girl whose passionate nature sooner or later
feels urgent desires, which are fed by the flatteries of men.
All her former pleasures little by little become stale; until she
finally meets a man to whom she is irresistibly drawn by a
strange, unfamiliar feeling, a man on whom she now stakes
all her hopes, forgetting the world around her, hearing nothing, seeing nothing, feeling nothing but him alone, longing
for him alone. Unspoiled by the shallow pleasures of an inconstant vanity, her desire draws her straight to one
goal—she wants to be his, to find in a lasting union all the
happiness she has missed, to experience all her yearned-for
joy. His repeated promises give certainty to her hope; his
bold caresses inflame her desire and hold her whole being in
a state of suspense, in anticipation of some supreme delights.
She works herself up to the highest pitch of excitement and
finally, when she opens her arms to embrace all her wishes—
her lover abandons her. Stunned, and almost out of her
mind, she finds herself above an abyss; all around her is
darkness; no way out, no consolation, no hope! The one person in whom she had found the center of her existence has

left her. She does not see the wide world spread out before her or the many others who might replace her loss; she feels herself alone, abandoned by all—and blindly hunted into a corner by the terrible agony of her heart, she throws herself into the depths to drown all her anguish in the embrace of death. —That, Albert, is the story of more than one; and now tell me, is not this a case like that of a disease? Nature is unable to fine a way out from the maze of confused and contradictory forces, and the patient must die.

"Shame on him who looks on and says: 'The foolish girl! If she had let time do its work, her despair would have lost its force, and very probably another man would have appeared willing to comfort her.' —This is exactly as if someone should say: 'The fool—to die of fever! If he had waited until he had recovered his strength, until the sap of life was improved, until the tumult in his blood had subsided, all would have been well, and he would still be alive today!' "

Albert, who had not quite grasped my comparison, had a few more objections to make, among them that, after all, I had only spoken of a simple girl. What he could not understand was how a person of intelligence, whose mind was not narrow, and who was capable of a larger view of things, could be exculpated. —"My friend," I exclaimed, "man is human, and the small amount of intelligence one may possess counts little or nothing against the rage of passion and the limits of human nature pressing upon him. Moreover—but of that another time," I said, and took my hat. Oh, my heart was so full! —And we parted without having understood each other. How difficult it is to understand one another in this world.

August 15

It is certainly true that nothing in the world makes a person indispensable but love. I feel that Lotte would not like to lose me, and the children have no other idea than that I should appear every morning. I went out there today to tune Lotte's clavichord but I did not get around to this task, for the children followed me everywhere, asking to be told a fairy tale, and Lotte herself begged me to do as they wished. I cut the bread for their supper, which they now take from me as eagerly as from Lotte, and told them their favorite story of the princess who was served by ghostly hands. I am learning a good deal from all this, I assure you; and I am amazed what an impression I make. When I sometimes have to invent a small detail which I forget the next time, they at once tell me that the story was different at the previous telling; so now I practice reciting it without alterations from beginning to end, like a chant. This has taught me what harm an author necessarily does to his book in a second revised edition, even though it may gain in poetic merit thereby. The very first impression finds us receptive; and we are so made that we can be convinced of the most incredible things; but these fix themselves immediately in our mind, and woe to him who would erase and eliminate them.

August 18

Must it so be that whatever makes man happy must later become the source of his misery?

That generous and warm feeling for living Nature which flooded my heart with such bliss, so that I saw the world around me as a Paradise, has now become an unbearable torment, a sort of demon that persecutes me wherever I go. When I formerly looked from the rock far across the river and the fertile valleys to the distant hills, and saw everything on all sides sprout and spring forth—the mountains covered with tall, thick trees from base to summit, the valleys winding between pleasant shading woods, the gently flowing river gliding among the whispering reeds and reflecting light clouds which sailed across the sky under the mild evening breeze; when I listened to the birds that bring the forest to life, while millions of midges danced in the red rays of a setting sun whose last flare roused the buzzing beetle from the grass; and all the whirring and weaving around me drew my attention to the ground underfoot where the moss, which wrests its nourishment from my hard rock, and the broom plant, which grows on the slope of the arid sand hill, revealed to me the inner, glowing, sacred life of Nature—how fervently did I take all this into my warm heart, feeling like a god in that overflowing abundance, while the beautiful forms of the infinite universe stirred and inspired my soul. Huge mountains surrounded me, precipices opened before me, and torrents gushed downward; the rivers streamed below, and wood and mountains sang; and I saw them at their mutual work of creation in the depths of the earth, all these unfathomable forces. And above the earth and below the sky swarms the variety of creatures, multifarious and multiform. Everything, everything populated with a thousand shapes; and mankind, huddled together in the security of its little houses, nesting throughout and dominating the wide world in its own way. Poor fool who belittles everything because you are yourself so small! From the inaccessible mountains, across the wasteland untrod by human foot, to the end of the unexplored seas breathes the spirit of the eternal Creator who rejoices in every atom of dust that divines Him and lives. —Oh, the times when I longed to fly on the crane's wings, as it passed overhead, to the shores of the illimitable ocean, in order to drink from the foaming cup of the Infinite an elating sensation of life, and to feel, if only for a moment, in the cramped forces of my being one drop of the bliss of that Being who creates everything in and through Himself.

My friend, only the memory of those hours eases my heart. Even the effort to recall and to express again in words those inexpressible sensations lifts my soul above itself, but also intensifies the anguish of my present state.

It is as if a curtain has been drawn away from my soul, and the scene of unending life is transformed before my eyes into the pit of the forever-open grave. Can you say: "This is!" when everything passes, everything rolls past with the speed of lightning and so rarely exhausts the whole power of its existence, alas, before it is swept away by the current, drowned and smashed on the rocks? There is not one moment which does not consume you and yours, and not one moment when you yourself are not inevitably destructive; the most harmless walk costs the lives of thousands of poor, minute worms; *one* step of your foot annihilates the painstaking constructions of ants, and stamps a small world into its ignominious grave. Ha! It is not the notable catastrophes of the world, the floods that wash away our villages, the earthquakes that swallow up our town which move me; my heart is instead worn out by the consuming power latent in the whole of Nature which has formed nothing that will not destroy its neighbor and itself. So I stagger with anxiety, Heaven and Earth and their weaving powers around me! I see nothing but an eternally devouring and ruminating monster.

August 21

In vain do I stretch my arms out for her in the morning, when I try to arouse myself from troubled dreams; in vain do I seek her at night in my bed, deluded by some happy and innocent dream in which I am sitting beside her in the meadow, holding her hand and covering it with a thousand kisses. And when, still heavy with sleep, I grope for her and suddenly find myself fully awake, a torrent of tears bursts from my oppressed heart, and I weep bitterly in view of a hopeless future.

August 22

It is disastrous, Wilhelm! All my energies are tuned to another pitch, have changed to a restless inactivity; I cannot be idle and yet at the same time cannot set to work at anything. My power of imagination fails me; I am insensible to Nature, and I am sick of books. If we fail ourselves, everything fails us. I swear that I should sometimes like to be a workman so that I could see, when I wake up in the morning, some prospect for the coming day, some impetus, some hope. I often envy Albert, whom I see buried up to his ears in documents; and I imagine that I should be better off were I in his place. Already more than once the thought of writing to you and to the Minister flashed through my mind, in order to apply for the post at the Legation which, you have assured me, I would not be refused. So I myself believe. The Minister has liked me for a long time, and has freqeuntly urged me to devote myself to some work; and sometimes, for an hour or so, it seems the thing to do. But when I come to consider it a little later, I remember the fable of the horse which, tired of its freedom, let itself be saddled and harnessed and was ridden to death. I don't know what to do. And, my dear fellow, isn't my longing for a change in my situation an innate, uneasy impatience that will pursue me wherever I go?

August 28

One thing is certain; if my disease could be cured, these people would cure it. Today is my birthday, and very early in the morning I received a little parcel from Albert. When I opened it I saw immediately one of the bows of pink ribbon Lotte had been wearing when I first met her and which I had often implored her to give me. The parcel also contained two books in duodecimo: the small Homer printed by Wetstein, which I had often wished to possess, so that I should not have to drag about with me on my walks the large volume edited by Ernesti. You see! that is how they anticipate my wishes, how well they select the small tokens of friendship which are a thousand times more precious than the dazzling presents which humiliate us, betraying the vanity of the giver. I kiss the ribbon over and over again and drink in with every breath the memory of the few blissful moments in those happy and irretrievable days. Wilhelm, so it is, and I do not complain—the blossoms of life are only phantoms. How many fade, leaving no trace behind; how few bear fruit, and how few of these fruits ripen! But still enough are left; but still—O my brother! should we neglect the ripe fruit, refuse to enjoy it, and let it rot?

Farewell! It is a glorious summer, and I often sit up in the trees of Lotte's orchard and take down with a long pole the pears from the highest branches. She stands below and catches them when I lower the pole.

August 30

Unhappy man! are you not a fool? Do you not deceive yourself? To what use is this endless raging passion? I have no prayers left except prayers to her; my imagination calls up no other image than hers, and I see everything in the world only in relation to her. And thus I spend many happy hours—until I must again tear myself from her. O Wilhelm, what things my heart urges me to do! After I have been with her for two or three hours, delighting in her form, her bearing, in the heavenly expressiveness of what she says, my nerves slowly become tense, my eyes grow dim, my ears no longer take in her words; and it seems as if an assassin had clutched me fast by the throat; if then my wildly beating heart tries to relieve my oppression but only succeeds in increasing my confusion—Wilhelm, in such moments I often do not know if I am indeed in this world. And if melancholy did not sometimes take hold of me, and Lotte grant me the poor comfort of crying my eyes out over her hand, I have to leave; I must get into the open air; I roam about in the fields. To climb a steep mountain is then my joy, working my way through pathless forest, through thickets which bruise me and thorns which tear me. Then I feel some relief. Some! And when I sink to the ground tired and thirsty, or sit on a fallen tree in the lonely forest, in the dead of night, when the full moon hangs over me, to give my wounded feet some relief, and then slip away in a calm sleep of exhaustion in the half-light—O Wilhelm! the solitude of a cell, the hairshirt and the spiked belt would be sweet comfort to my yearning heart. Adieu! I see no end to this misery except in the grave.

September 3

I must go! Thank you, Wilhelm, for having confirmed me in my wavering decision. For two weeks I have been constantly thinking of leaving her. I must go. She is again in the town, staying with a friend. And Albert—and—I must go!

September 10

What a night it has been, Wilhelm! And now I can endure anything. I shall not see her again. Oh, if I could only fall on your neck and describe with a thousand joyous tears all the emotions that are storming in my heart. Here I sit, gasping for breath, trying to calm down, and waiting for the morning to come; horses are ordered for sunrise.

And she sleeps peacefully and does not know that she will never see me again. I have torn myself away and was strong enough not to betray my intention while we talked together for two hours. Good God, what a conversation it was!

Albert had promised me to be in the garden with Lotte immediately after supper. I stood on the terrace under the tall chestnut trees and watched the sun, which was, for me, setting for the last time over the lovely valley and the gentle river. I had so often stood here with her, looking at the beautiful scene, and now—I paced up and down the avenue that was so dear to me. I had often been drawn to this place by a secret impulse before I even knew Lotte; and how delighted we had been when, at the beginning of our acquaintance, we discovered our mutual liking for the place, which is really one of the most romantic I have ever seen planned by art.

First you have the wide view between the chestnut trees—but, I remember having already written you a great deal about it, how one is soon closed in by high screens of beech

trees, and how the avenue grows darker and darker, because
of the adjoining shrubbery, until at last all ends in a secluded
little circle, around which a thrilling solitude hovers. I can
still feel the odd sensation which touched me when I first
entered it at high noon; I had a faint presentiment of the
kind of setting it would make for both happiness and pain.

I had indulged in these sweet and yearning thoughts of
parting and reunion for almost half an hour, when I heard
them coming up the terrace. I ran to meet them, took Lotte's
hand and kissed it with deep emotion. We had just reached
the top of the terrace when the moon rose behind the
wooded hill; we talked of various things and approached,
before we knew it, the somber recess. Lotte entered and sat
down, Albert beside her, as I did too, but my inner restlessness did not allow me to remain seated for long; I stood up,
stood in front of them, paced to and fro, and again sat down:
it was an agonizing situation. Lotte drew our attention to the
beautiful effect of moonlight illuminating the whole length
of the terrace before us, which opened where the screening
beech trees ended: a lovely sight, the more striking because
complete darkness closed us in on all sides. We were silent,
until she said, after a time: "I never take a moonlight walk,
never, without thinking of my dear lost ones; without being
overawed by the sense of death and of future life. We shall
live," she went on, her voice vibrating with the most beautiful emotion, "but, Werther, shall we find one another again
and know one another? What do you feel? What do you
say?"

"Lotte," I said, giving her my hand as my eyes filled with tears, "we shall meet again, here and beyond." My voice failed me. Wilhelm, did she have to ask me that when my heart was in anguish because of our coming separation!

"And I wonder if our dear lost ones know about us," she continued, "if they feel that we remember them with warm affection when everything goes well with us? Oh, the image of my mother is always with me when I sit among her children, my children, on a quiet evening, and they gather around me as they used to gather around her, and then I look up to Heaven with longing and tears, and wish that she might for a moment look in on us and see how I have kept my promise given to her in the hour of her death: to be a mother to her children. With what feeling I then cry out: 'Forgive me, dearest Mother, if I am not to them what you were. Oh, do I not do everything I can; are they not dressed and fed and, what is more, cared for and loved? Could you only see the harmony among us, dear sainted Mother, you would thank with fervent gratitude the God whom you implored with your last bitter tears to protect your children.'"

These were her words! O Wilhelm, who can repeat what she said? How can dead cold written words convey the heavenly flower of her soul? Albert gently interrupted her: "Dear Lotte, this affects you too much. I know that your soul is immersed in these ideas, but I implore you—" "O Albert!" she replied, "I know you have not forgotten those evenings when we sat together at the small round table, when Father was away on a journey, and we had sent the little ones to bed. You often had a good book with you, but you seldom had time to read. Was not the association with her exquisite soul worth more than anything else? The beautiful, gentle, cheerful and always active woman! God alone knows how often, in my bed, I have prayed in tears that He might make me her equal."

"Lotte," I cried, kneeling before her and taking her hand, which I covered with tears, "Lotte, the blessing of God rests upon you, and the spirit of your mother." — "If you had only known her," she said, and pressed my hand. "She was worthy to be known by you." I almost fainted. Never had anything more magnificent, more exalting, been said about me. She continued: "And this woman had to die in the flower of her years, when her youngest son was only six months old. Her illness was not a long one; she was calm and resigned, and she worried only about her children, especially the youngest. When her end drew near, she said to me: 'Send them up to me!' and I brought them into her room— the little one, who did not understand, and the older ones, who were very much upset; they stood around her bed and she raised her hands and prayed over them, then kissed one after the other and sent them away, saying to me: 'Be their mother!' I gave her my hand and promised. —'You promise a great deal, my daughter,' she said, 'both the heart of a mother and the eye of a mother. I have often seen from your grateful tears that you feel what that means. Feel this for your sisters and brothers, and for your father the loyalty and obedience of a wife. You will comfort him.' She asked to see him, but he had left the house to hide his unbearable grief—he was completely broken.

"Albert, you were in the room with us. She had heard someone walking about, and asked who it was, and called you to her side. How she looked at you and at me, her mind relieved and at rest, knowing that we would be happy, be happy together." Albert took Lotte in his arms and kissed her, crying: "We are! We shall be!" The usually imperturbable Albert was shaken, and I was beside myself.

"Werther," she began, "and this woman had to die! Dear God! When I sometimes think that the dearest thing in our lives was taken away, and that no one felt it as keenly as the children, who complained for a long time afterward that the black men had carried away their mother!"

She stood up, and I woke, shaken, from my trance, but remained seated, still holding her hand. "We must go," she said, "it is late." She tried to withdraw her hand, but I held it all the more firmly. "We shall meet again," I exclaimed, "we shall find one another, and know one another under whatever form. I am going away," I went on. "I go voluntarily, but if I should have to say 'Forever' I could not bear it. Farewell, Lotte! Farewell, Albert! We shall meet again." — "Yes, tomorrow, I suppose," she replied lightly. How I felt that word "tomorrow"! Oh, she was unsuspecting, when she drew her hand away. —They walked down the avenue; I stood in the moonlight, looking after them; then I flung myself on the ground and wept until my tears were exhausted, sprang up again and ran out on the terrace, where I still could catch a glimpse of her white dress moving in the shadow of the tall linden trees near the garden gate. I stretched out my arms, and it disappeared.

◄ Book Two ►

We arrived here yesterday. The envoy is indisposed and will, therefore, stay at home for a few days. If he were not so disagreeable, all would be well. I feel that Destiny has some hard tests in store for me. But I won't lose courage! A light heart can bear anything! A light heart? I laugh when those words come from my pen. Oh, a little more lightheartedness would make me the happiest being under the sun. What! With others around me of scanty talent and ability, bragging in complacent self-content, should I despair of my abilities and gifts? Good Lord, you who presented me with all these, why did You not keep half, and give me instead self-confidence and contentment!

Patience! Patience! Things will improve. For, my dear friend, I admit that you were right. Since I have been seeing all sorts of people day in and day out, and have observed how they carry on, I am more lenient with myself. It is true that we are so made that we compare everything with ourselves and ourselves with everything. Therefore, our fortune or misfortune depends on the objects and persons to which we compare ourselves; and for that reason nothing is more dangerous than solitude. Our imagination, by its nature inclined to exalt itself, and nourished by the fantastic imagery of poetry, creates a series of beings of which we are the lowest, so that everything else appears more wonderful, everyone else more perfect. And that is completely natural. We so frequently feel that we are lacking in many qualities which another person apparently possesses; and we then furnish such a person with everything we ourselves possess and with a certain idealistic complacency in addition. And in this fashion a Happy Being is finished to perfection—the creature of our imagination.

If, on the other hand, we just continue to do our best in spite of weakness and hard work, we very often find that, with all our delaying and tacking about, we achieve more than others with their sailing and rowing—and—it gives us a true feeling of our worth if we keep pace with others or even overtake them.

November 26

I begin rather to enjoy myself. The best feature is that there is enough work to do, and that the variety of people, the many new characters, form a colorful drama for my spirit. I have made the acquaintance of Count C., a man I am forced to admire more every day; an intelligent, broad-minded man who has not become cold through his quickness of perception, but radiates a great feeling of friendship and affection. He showed an interest in me when I had to deliver a message; from my first words he saw that we understood each other and that he could talk with me as he could not with everyone. I cannot praise sufficiently his candid manner with me. Nothing in this world equals the warm pleasure we take in seeing a great mind opening to us.

December 24

The envoy annoys me greatly, as I knew he would. He is the most meticulous fool that ever lived, proceeding step by step and fussing like an old maid; a man who is never satisfied with his own work, and consequently never satisfied with another's. I do my work quickly and like to leave things written down as they come; but he is capable of returning my memorandum to me, saying: "It is good, but better look through it once more; one is always able to find a better word, a more precise particle." It's enough to drive one mad! —No "and," not the smallest conjunction, must be omitted; and he is a deadly enemy of the inversions that sometimes slip from my pen. If one does not reel off his periods to the traditional tune, he does not understand one word of them. It is a burden to have to work with such a man.

The confidence of Count C. is my only compensation. The other day he told me quite frankly how dissatisfied he is with the slowness and pedantry of the envoy. "That type of person makes things difficult for himself as well as for others. But," he added, "one has to resign oneself like a traveler who has to cross a mountain; of course, if the mountain were not there, the journey would be much shorter and easier; but there it is, and one has to scale it!"

My old gentleman also sensed in a way that the Count prefers me to him and that vexes and annoys him, so that he seizes any opportunity to disparage the Count in my presence. I, of course, contradict him and only make matters worse. Yesterday I even lost my temper, for his words were meant for me, as well, when he said: "The Count is quite good at worldly affairs, because he works quickly and has a fluent pen, but, like all literary people, he lacks solid erudition." He then grimaced, as though to say: "Do you feel the prick?" But it had no effect on me; I felt only contempt for a man capable of so thinking and behaving. I held my ground and parried with considerable heat. I said that the Count was a man one had to respect for both his character and his knowledge. "I have never met anyone," I continued, "whose range of interests is so wide, and who yet expends so much energy on matters of ordinary life." This was all Greek to him, and I took leave, not wishing to be choked by more gall and having to listen to further nonsense.

And all this I owe to you, who talked me into assuming this yoke, and harped so much on activity. Activity! If it is true that the man who plants potatoes, or rides into town to sell his grain, is not doing more than I, then I shall slave for another ten years on this galley to which I am at present chained.

And the splendid misery, the boredom among the horrid people who are assembled here! Their social ambitions, the way they watch and spy on one another in order to gain another tiny step; their most contemptible passions flaunted without any reticence. One woman, for instance, tells everyone about her nobility and her native country, so that every stranger is forced to think: "This woman is a fool to pride herself on that little bit of nobility and on her country's fame." But, to make it worse, the woman is in reality the daughter of a district clerk from this very region. You see, I cannot understand the human race when it has so little judgment and prostitutes itself in such a vulgar way.

In fact, I realize each day more clearly, dear friend, how foolish it is to judge others by oneself. And as I am so preoccupied with myself, and since this heart of mine is so stormy, oh, how gladly would I let others go their way if they would only let me go mine!

What irritates me most of all are the disgraceful social conditions. I know, of course, as well as anyone, how necessary class distinctions are, and how many advantages I myself gain from them; but they should not stand in my way just when I might enjoy some little pleasure, some gleam of joy on this earth. The other day, on a walk, I made the acquaintance of Fräulein von B., a charming creature, who has preserved a great naturalness in the midst of this stiff and conventional life. We were very congenial as we talked, and when we separated I asked permission to visit her. She consented so frankly that I could hardly wait for the proper moment to make my call. She does not come from these parts and lives in the house of an aunt. I thoroughly disliked the old lady's looks, but I showed her much attention and, for the most part, turned the conversation in her direction. In less than half an hour I guessed almost all that the girl later confirmed: namely, that her dear old aunt lacked everything, having neither a decent fortune nor any wits, and no prop but her family tree, and was protected only by her noble rank, behind which she had entrenched herself and enjoyed the last pleasure left her: to look down from her height on the heads of the burghers. They say she was very beautiful in her youth and frittered away her life, at first by tormenting many a poor young man with her whims; but in middle age obediently submissive to the domination of an old officer who, in exchange for this submission and a moderate dowry, spent the Bronze Age with her, and died. She now finds herself alone in the Iron Age; and no one would pay any attention to her if her niece were not so charming.

January 8, 1772

What dreadful people there are, whose minds are completely absorbed in matters of etiquette, whose thoughts and aspirations all year long turn over the single problem how to push oneself one chair higher at table. And it is not as though they had nothing else to do. No, on the contrary, work continues to pile up because trivial annoyances hinder the dispatch of more important matters. Last week a quarrel started during a sleighing party and the whole fun was spoiled.

The fools, who do not understand that actual rank does not matter at all and that he who occupies the top very rarely plays the chief role. How often a king is ruled by a minister; how many ministers by their secretaries! And who is then the first? I believe it is the man who knows his fellow-men at a glance and has sufficient power or shrewdness to harness their forces and passions to the execution of his plans.

January 20

I must write you, dear Lotte, here in the taproom of a poor country inn, where I have taken refuge from a heavy storm. Since the time I have been a stranger wandering around in D., that depressing hole of a town, among strangers to my heart, there has not been one moment, not one, when my heart would have told me to write you; but now, in this hovel, this solitary narrow place, while snow and hail pelt on my little window, my first thought is of you. The moment I entered, your image, the memory of you, suddenly overwhelmed me, O Lotte, so sacred and so warm! Dear God, it was the first happy moment in a long time.

If you could see me, my dear, in the flood of distractions! How dried up my senses are getting to be; not for one minute does my heart overflow—not one blissful hour! Nothing! Nothing! I seem to be standing before a sort of raree show, watching the little men and little horses jerk before my eyes; and I often ask myself if everything is not an optical illusion. I join in the play or, rather, I am moved about like a marionette, and sometimes, when I grasp the wooden hand of my neighbor, I shrink back with a shudder. Every evening I plan to enjoy the sunrise, and each morning I fail to get up. During the day I look forward to the moonlight, but later I stay in my room. I do not even know why I get up or why I go to bed.

The leaven which set my life in motion is wanting; the charm which kept me awake far into the night and roused me from my sleep in the morning is gone.

I have found only one feminine friend here: a Fräulein von B., who resembles you, dear Lotte, if anyone can possibly resemble you. "Well, well!" you will say, "this fellow resorts to pretty compliments!" There is some truth in it, I have lately been very gallant, which is, after all, my nature to be. I have been very witty, and the ladies say that no one can flatter as well as I (or tell lies, you will add, because one cannot flatter without lying, you see). But I wanted to talk about Fräulein von B. She has a great deal of spirit, which shines out from her blue eyes. Her high rank is a burden to her, as it does not satisfy any of the desires of her heart. She longs to escape from the turmoil, and we spend hours with fantasies of country scenes filled with pure happiness; ah, and of you! How often must she do homage to you! She is not compelled to—she does it voluntarily, loves to hear about you, and loves you.

I wish that I could be sitting at your feet in the dear, familiar room, with our little ones dancing about us; and if they became too noisy, I could gather them around me and quiet them with a frightening fairy tale.

The sun is sinking in full glory over the dazzling snow-white countryside; the storm has passed, and I—must return to my cage. Adieu! Is Albert with you? And how—? God forgive me that question!

February 8

For a week we have had the most horrible weather, but for me it is a blessing. As long as I have been here, there has not been one fine day that has not been spoiled or ruined for me by someone. Now, when it pours, and drizzles, and freezes, and thaws, I think—well, it cannot be worse inside than it is out of doors, or vice versa; and that is good. When the sun rises in the morning and promises a fine day, I can never resist exclaiming, "Now they again have a heavenly gift which they can spoil for one another." Nothing exists that these people cannot spoil for one another. Health, reputation, happiness, recreation! And all this largely through silliness, stupidity, and narrow-mindedness. Sometimes I feel like imploring them on my knees not to rage so violently against themselves.

February 17

I fear that my envoy and I will not be together much longer. That man is absolutely unbearable. His way of working and of handling affairs is so ridiculous that I cannot restrain myself from contradicting him; and I often handle some matter at my will and in my own way—a way, of course, which he always disapproves. For this reason he has recently complained of me at Court, and the Minister reproved me, although mildly; but still it was a reproof; and I was about to send in my resignation when I received a personal letter from him—a letter that brought me down on my knees in admiration of its generous, wise, and noble feeling. He puts my extreme sensitiveness in the right place, although he credits my exaggerated ideas of efficiency, of influence upon others, of more intelligent management of business, as youthful and praiseworthy courage; and he does not wish to eradicate these ideas but to temper them, and lead them into the right direction where they can be sure of producing a powerful effect. I am now fortified for a week, and have found my balance again. Peace of mind is a wonderful thing, as is pleasure in oneself. Dear friend, if only these treasures were not so fragile as they are precious and beautiful.

February 20

God bless you, dear friends, and give you all the happy days of which I am deprived.

Thank you, Albert, for having kept me in the dark. I was waiting for news about the day of your wedding and had intended on that day solemnly to take down Lotte's silhouette from my wall and bury it among other papers. Now you are a married couple, and her silhouette is still there. Well, it shall stay there! And why not? I know that I am still with you; that I remain in Lotte's heart without doing any harm to you; I have—yes, I have the second place in it, and will and must keep that place. Oh, I should go mad if she were able to forget—Albert, Hell lies in that thought. Albert, farewell! Farewell, angel from Heaven! Farewell, Lotte!

Something has so humiliated me that I shall be forced to leave this place, and I gnash my teeth! The Devil! The harm is done, and it is *your* fault alone—*you* spurred me on, pushed and tormented me into accepting a position that was not congenial to me. Well, here I am! and you have had your way! And in order to prevent you from telling me that it was my eccentric ideas which ruined everything, I here recount, dear sir, the story, plain and clear, as a chronicler would put it down.

Count C. is very fond of me and singles me out, as is well known, and as I have written you many times. He had invited me for dinner at his house yesterday, on the very day when the whole aristocratic set, ladies and gentlemen, are accustomed to meet there late in the evening. I had completely forgotten this fact; and it also did not occur to me that subordinate officials like myself are not welcome on such occasions. Very well. I dined with the Count, and afterward we walked up and down the great hall in conversation and were joined later by Colonel B.; so the hour of the party drew near. God knows, I did not suspect anything. Then the more-than-gracious Lady S. entered with her spouse and her nobly hatched little goose of a flat-bosomed and tight-laced daughter. *En passant,* they opened their eyes wide and turned up their noses in the traditional highly aristocratic manner. As that clique is entirely repulsive to me, I had decided to leave, only waiting until the Count could free himself from trivial chatter, when Fräulein von B. entered the room. Since I become always a little more cheerful when I see her, I stayed on, took my place behind her chair, and noticed only after some time had passed that she was not talking to me with her usual frankness but with some embarrassment. This took me by surprise. "Is she really like the rest of these people?" I asked myself and was piqued. I wanted to leave, but stayed on, because I should have liked to free her from a blame I did not believe, and still hoped for a kind word from her and—whatever you wish. Meanwhile, more and more people were filling the room. Baron F. all gotten up in a complete outfit dating back to the coronation of Francis I, Hofrat R. (but here *in qualitate* called Herr von N.) with his deaf wife, not to mention the badly-reduced-in-circumstances J., who had patched up the worn places in his old-fashioned clothes with brand-new material—all these people kept arriving in swarms; and I spoke to some of those I knew who were, however, very laconic, I thought—and paid attention only to my Fräulein von B. I did not notice that the dames at the far end of the room were whispering into each other's ears or that this whispering spread to the gentlemen; that Lady S. was talking to the Count (Fräulein von B. recounted all this to me afterward), until he finally came up to me and drew me into a window recess. "You know our strange social conventions," he said, "and I notice that the company is displeased to see you here, although I should not want you, for anything in the world—"

— "Your Excellency!" I interrupted, "I apologize exceedingly; I should have thought of this before, and I know you will forgive me my inconsequence. I wanted to leave some time ago, but a malicious spirit held me back," I added, smiling and bowing to him. The Count pressed my hand with a warmth that expressed everything. I turned my back on the illustrious company, slipped away and took a cabriolet to M., to see the sunset from the hill, while reading in Homer the magnificent passage which describes how Odysseus is entertained by the faithful swineherd. All this was perfect.

In the evening I returned to the inn for supper. There were only a few people in the taproom, playing at dice at the corner of a table, having turned back the tablecloth. The honest Adelin then came in, put down his hat when he saw me, and, coming up closer, said to me in a low voice: "Did something annoy you?" "Annoy me?" I said. — "The Count asked you to leave his party." — "The Devil take it!" I said. "I was glad to get out into the fresh air." — "Good that you take it so lightly," he said. "The thing that worries me is that everyone is already talking." Now for the first time the whole thing began to irritate me. I imagined that everyone who came in for supper glanced at me and seemed to know about the incident. My blood was up.

And today when everyone pities me wherever I go and when I hear that my triumphant rivals are saying, "You see where arrogance leads, when proud people who boast of their little share of brains think they can ignore all conventions" (and whatever else these gossiping dogs may invent), one would like to take a knife and plunge it into one's heart; for, whatever one may say about independence, I should like to see the person who can allow rascals to slander him when they have the upper hand. When it is only empty talk, it is easy to ignore them.

March 16

Everything is against me. Today I met Fräulein von B. in the avenue. I could not keep myself from speaking to her; to tell her, as soon as we were at some distance from her companions, how much she had hurt me the other day. "O Werther," she said with deep feeling, "how could you, knowing my heart, interpret my confusion in such a way? How I suffered for you from the moment I entered the room! I foresaw everything, and a warning word was on the tip of my tongue a dozen times. I knew that Lady S. and Lady T. would leave with their husbands rather than remain while you were there; and I knew that the Count cannot risk their displeasure—and now all this scandal!" — "What do you mean?" I asked, concealing my alarm, because everything that Adelin had told me the previous day made me suddenly feel very uneasy. — "How much it has already cost me," said the sweet creature with tears in her eyes. —I was no longer master of myself, and was ready to throw myself at her feet. "Do tell me the truth," I cried. The tears ran down her cheeks, and I was almost out of my mind. She dried her tears without trying to conceal them. "You know my aunt," she began. "She was at the party and with her keen eyes kept a close watch on everything. Werther, I had to suffer for it last night, and this morning I was given a lecture on my friendship with you, and was forced to listen to the degrading, discrediting things she said about you, and could not—was not allowed to—defend you half as much as I wished."

Every word she spoke pierced my heart like a sword. She did not sense how charitable it would have been to keep all this from me; and she went on to say that more gossip would soon begin to run wild, and mentioned the sort of people who would gloat over it. How delighted they all would be about the punishment I had received for my arrogance and haughty contempt toward others, for which they had often blamed me. All this, Wilhelm, I had to hear from her, spoken in a tone of sincerest sympathy. I was completely crushed, and am still furious. I wish that someone would have the courage to blame me openly so that I could thrust my dagger through his body; if I saw blood, I should certainly feel better. Today I have taken up a knife a dozen times, intending to relieve with it my suffocating heart. I have been told that a noble breed of horses, when overheated and hunted almost to death, will by instinct bite open a vein and so recover their breath. I often feel the same. I should like to open one of my veins and gain eternal freedom for myself.

March 24

I have sent in my resignation to the Court, and I hope that it will be accepted. You will forgive me for not asking your permission first. It is absolutely necessary for me to leave; and everything you will say, to persuade me to stay, I myself know. And therefore—sugar the bitter pill for my mother. I cannot help myself, and she must put up with the fact that I cannot help her either. Of course, it is going to hurt her. To see the beginning brilliant career of her son, which might have mounted, perhaps, to the office of privy councilor and envoy, stop so suddenly, and the little horse brought back to its stable! Now think of the matter as you will and try to figure out the possible conditions under which I might and should have stayed. Enough, I am going. But that you may know where I am going, let me tell you that Prince ——, who likes my company extremely, when he heard of my intention, invited me to accompany him to his estates, and to spend the lovely springtime there. He has promised that I will be completely left alone, and as we understand one another very well, up to a certain point, I shall take my chance and go with him.

❧ Postscript ❧

Thank you for both your letters. I have not answered them because I kept back the enclosed note until my resignation had been accepted by the Court. I was afraid that my mother would appeal to the Minister and frustrate my decision. But now everything has been settled, and my discharge has been signed. I can't tell you how reluctantly it was granted, and what the Minister wrote me; you would burst into fresh laments. The hereditary prince sent me twenty-five ducats as a farewell gift, with a note which moved me to tears. Therefore I do not need the money from my mother, for which I asked her the other day.

May 5

I leave here tomorrow, and, as my birthplace is only six miles
away from my route, I want to visit it again and indulge in
the memory of former happy days. I plan to enter the town
by the same gate through which my mother drove out with
me when she left the dear familiar place after the death of
my father to shut herself in the unbearable town where she
now lives. Adieu, Wilhelm; you are going to hear from me
about my journey.

May 9

I have ended the pilgrimage to my native town with all the
devotion of a pilgrim, and many unexpected emotions have
taken hold of me. I asked the postilion to stop beside the tall
linden tree, fifteen minutes from the town, on the road to S.
There I got out and ordered him to drive on, as I wished to
walk and to enjoy every memory in a new and vivid way to
my heart's content. There I now stood under the linden tree
which was once the goal and boundary of my walks as a boy.
How different from the present moment! In those days, in
my happy ignorance, my greatest desire had been to get
away, out into the unknown world, where I hoped to find all
the joy and all the satisfaction possible for my aspiring and

yearning heart. Now I had come back from that wide world
—oh, my friend, with so many shattered hopes, so many
ruined plans. I saw before me the mountains which had so
many times been the goal of my desires. I used to sit here for
hours, longing to be beyond, completely absorbed, heart and
soul, in those woods, those valleys which appeared to my eyes
so pleasant and mysterious. If I knew that I had to return
home at a certain hour, how I loathed leaving the beloved
spot! —As I approached the town, I greeted all the familiar
little garden houses, but heartily disliked the newer ones, as
well as all the other changes that had been made. I entered
by the town gate; and now I knew my way again at once.
Dear friend, I'll not go into any details; for, delightful as
they are, such a detailed description might be monotonous. I
had planned to take a room overlooking the market place,
next to our old house. As I walked in that direction I noticed
that the school, wherein a conscientious old dame had
penned up our childhood, had been turned into a shop. I
vividly remembered the restlessness, the tears, the dullness of
mind, the anxiety of heart, that I suffered in that hole. Every
single step I took stirred up memories. No pilgrim in the
Holy Land could come across so many places of religious
memory, or have a soul more filled with pious emotion.
—Another example among thousands: I went down along
the river to a certain farm, where formerly I had often
walked. This was the place where we boys used to compete,
skimming flat stones which skipped along the surface of the
water. I clearly remembered how often I stood there, follow-

ing the river with my eyes, with strange presentiments in my heart; how colorfully my imagination painted the countries through which the river flowed, and how soon I discovered that my imagination had limits. Still I knew that the river ran on and on, and I completely lost myself in the vision of an unseen far country. —You see, dear friend, how limited and how happy were the glorious Ancients! how naïve their emotions and their poetry! When Ulysses speaks of the immeasurable sea and the infinite earth, everything is true, human, deeply felt, intimate, and mysterious. What is the use of my present knowledge, which I share with any schoolboy, that the earth is round? Man needs only a few clods of earth whereon to enjoy himself, and even fewer for his last rest.

Here I am in the Prince's hunting lodge. Life with this gentleman goes along very well, for he is simple and sincere. But he is surrounded by a strange crowd of people whom I cannot understand at all. They are evidently not bad fellows, but they do not have the look of honest ones. Sometimes they make an honest impression on me, but I cannot bring myself to trust them. Another thing I regret is that the Prince often talks about matters he has only heard or read, and he then takes a position that some other person may have presented to him.

Besides, he admires my intelligence and my talents more than my heart, which is, after all, my only pride, and the fountainhead of all—all strength, happiness and misery. Anyone can know what I know. My heart alone is my own.

I had something on my mind which I did not want to tell you until it was carried out; now that nothing has come of it, it does not matter. I wanted to go to the war; that is what I have long had at heart. It was my chief reason for coming here with the Prince, who is a general in the —— service. During one of our walks I told him of my intention; he advised against it, and there would have had to be more passion in me than actually existed in my passing mood to have prevented me from listening to his arguments.

June 11

You can say what you will; I cannot stay here any longer. What is the use? Time hangs heavy on my hands. The Prince treats me very well, yet I do not feel on my own ground. Fundamentally, we have nothing in common. He is an intelligent man, but of the average kind; to talk to him is not too different from reading a well-written book. I shall stay another week and then take up my wandering again. My drawing is the best thing I have done here. The Prince has a feeling for art and might feel still more strongly in that direction if he were not limited by the pseudo-scientific approach and by trite terminology. I often get furious when I talk with him about Nature and Art with warmth and imagination, only to have him attempt to be clever as he stumbles in with some trite term.

June 16

It is true, I am only a wanderer, a pilgrim on this earth! But are you more?

June 18

Where do I want to go? I tell you in confidence that I must stay here another two weeks; and then I pretend to myself that I wish to visit the mines in ——. But, to tell you the truth, there is nothing in that. I only want to be closer to Lotte once more; that is all. And I mock at my heart—and do what it demands.

July 29

No, it is good! Everything is good! I—her husband! O God, who made me, if you had given me that unspeakable happiness, my whole life would be one perpetual prayer. I will not protest—forgive my tears, forgive my hopeless wishes! She— my wife! If I could have closed in my arms the loveliest creature under the sun— A shudder goes through my whole body, Wilhelm, when I see Albert put his arm around her slender waist.

And may I say it? Why not, Wilhelm? She would have been happier with me than with him. Oh, he is not the man to satisfy all the needs of her heart. A certain lack of sensitiveness, a certain lack of—call it as you will. —His heart does not beat in sympathy with, say, a passage in a favorite book, where my heart and Lotte's beat in the same rhythm; as on a hundred other occasions when our feelings about the action of a third person are in accord. Dear Wilhelm! It is true that he loves her with all his soul; and how much such a love deserves!

A most disagreeable person has interrupted me. My tears are dried. I am distracted. Adieu, dear friend.

August 4

I am not alone in suffering. The hopes of all men are shattered and their expectations betrayed. I went to see the good woman I met under the linden tree. Her older boy ran up to met me; his joyful shouts brought her near; she looked very downcast. Her first words were, "Kind sir, my little Hans is dead!" He was the youngest of her sons. I was silent. "And my husband," she went on, "has returned from Switzerland with empty pockets. If some kind people had not helped him, he would have been forced to beg. He caught a fever on the way." I did not know what to say. I gave something to the little one. She asked me to accept a few apples, which I did, and left this place of melancholy memory.

August 21

As quick as you turn your hand, so quickly everything has changed. Now and then a happier glimpse of life dawns for me, but, alas, only for a moment! —When I become lost in dreams I cannot avoid thinking, "What if Albert should die? You would! she would—" And then I begin to run after the chimera until it leads me to abysses from which I shrink back in horror.

When I walk out of the town gate, along the road over which I first drove to fetch Lotte to the ball, how changed it all is! Everything, everything is over! No visible trace of the past, not a heartbeat of my former emotion. I feel like a ghost must feel who returns to the burned and destroyed castle which he built in the flower of his youth and filled with splendid objects, and on his deathbed hopefully bequeathed to his beloved son.

Sometimes I cannot understand how another *can,* how he *dare* love her, since I alone love her completely and devotedly, knowing only her, and having nothing in the world but her!

Yes, it is so. As Nature declines toward autumn, autumn is in me and around me. My leaves are turning yellow, and already the leaves of the trees nearby have fallen. Did I not once write you, soon after I arrived here, of a certain peasant lad? I inquired about him again in Wahlheim, and was told that he had been turned out of service; but no one seemed to know his whereabouts. Yesterday I met him by chance on my way to another village; I spoke to him, and he told me his story, which moved me more than I can say, as you will easily understand when I repeat it to you. But why repeat it? Why do I not keep my grief and my anxiety to myself? Why should I worry you? Why do I always give you reason to deplore and to reprove me? Never mind! This may also be part of my destiny!

With subdued sadness, mingled with shyness, the lad answered my questions at first; but soon, as if he suddenly recognized himself and myself once more, he confessed to me with more confidence the mistakes he had made, and mourned over his misfortunes. Dear friend, if I could only lay before your judgment every word of his story! He confessed, in fact he told me with a sort of joyful reminiscence, that his passion for the woman who employed him had daily grown on him, to the degree that he finally had not known what to do; had not known, as he expressed it, which way to turn his head. He had not been able to eat, to drink or to sleep; he had felt as if something was choking him. He did what he was not supposed to do, and forgot what he had been ordered to do; it was as if an evil spirit drove him on, until one day, knowing the woman to be in an upper room, he had followed her, or rather had been drawn after her by some magic power. When she resisted his demands, he was about to use force; he did not know what happened to him, and God was his witness that his intentions toward her had always been honest, that his most ardent wish was that she might marry him and spend the rest of her life with him. — After having talked for a while, he began to falter, like a person who has something more to say but lacks the courage to speak out. At last he confessed rather timidly that she had allowed him a few small familiarities and had not grudged him some intimacies. He checked himself two or three times, again and again protesting emphatically that he did not mention this to defame her, as he put it; he loved and respected her as much as formerly; he had never mentioned the matter before to anyone and now told it to me only to convince me that he was not unnatural and not insane. And now, dear friend, you will again hear my old song, which I am forever repeating: if you could have seen this man as he stood before me, as he still stands before my mind! Could I but describe to you every exact detail so that you could understand what a warm interest I take—must take—in his destiny. But enough of this; as you know my destiny as well, as you know me as well, you will understand only too clearly what attracts me to all unfortunate beings, and particularly to this one.

As I re-read this letter, I see that I have forgotten to finish the story which you can, however, easily imagine for youself. The woman defended herself, and at this moment her brother came in. This brother had for a long time hated the lad and wished to have him out of the house, being afraid that his children would lose the inheritance of his childless sister if she should marry again (an inheritance they looked forward to with keen expectation). The woman's brother immediately showed him the door and raised such a hue and cry that the woman, even if she had wished to, could not well have taken him back into her service. She had now hired another farm hand; but this man, too, people said, had caused a definite break between the brother and herself; and she was expected almost certainly to marry this new man; but my lad said that he was determined to make an end of himself before that day.

What I recount to you here is not exaggerated or sentimentalized; indeed, I may say that I have told it poorly, very poorly, and vulgarized it, by telling it in our conventional moralizing phrases.

This kind of love, this fidelity, this passion, is, as you see, no poetic invention. It is alive; it exists in its purest form among those people whom we call uneducated and coarse. We educated people—miseducated into nothingness! Read this story with reverence, I beg you. Today I am calm while I write; you see from my handwriting that I do not scribble and scrawl as I usually do. Read, dearest friend, and bear in mind that you are reading the story of your friend as well. Yes, all this has happened to me, and will happen to me, and I am not as good-natured by half, or as determined as the poor wretch with whom I almost haven't the courage to compare myself.

September 5

She had written a little note to her husband, who was in the country attending to some business. It began: "Best and dearest of men! Come back as soon as you can; I await you with the utmost joy."—A friend came in and brought a message from Albert saying that he would be delayed because of some circumstance or other. Lotte's note was not sent; and I found it by chance in the evening. I read it and smiled; and she asked me why. "What a divine gift is imagination!" I exclaimed. "For a moment I could pretend to myself that this was written to me." —She did not reply and seemed displeased; and I fell silent.

September 6

I struggled with myself before I decided to discard my plain blue dress coat, which I wore when I first danced with Lotte; but it had become very shabby. I have had a new one made, exactly like the first, down to collar and lapels; and also another yellow waistcoat and a pair of breeches.

But the effect is not quite the same. I don't know—it may be that in time I shall like it better.

September 12

She has been away for a few days to meet Albert and return with him. Today, when I came into her room, she was back and welcomed me; and I kissed her hand with great delight.

A canary flew down from the mirror and perched on her shoulder. "A new friend," she said, and called him to her hand. "It is a present for my little ones. How sweetly he behaves! Look at him! When I give him a crumb of bread, he flutters his wings and pecks so daintily. He also kisses me. Look!"

When she offered her sweet lips to the little bird, he nestled closely to them, as though he could feel the happiness given to him.

"He shall kiss you, too," she said, handing the bird over to me. The tiny beak made its way from her lips to mine, and the pecking touch was like a breath—a foretaste of the pleasures of love.

"His kiss is not without greed," I said. "He looks for food and flies back, not satisfied with an empty caress."

"He also takes food from my mouth," she said. She offered some crumbs to the bird with her lips, which smiled with the happiness of innocently sympathizing love.

I turned my eyes away. She should not do this! She should not inflame my imagination with these pictures of heavenly innocence and joy and arouse my heart from the sleep into which the monotony of life often lulls it. But why not? She trusts me so implicitly! She knows how much I love her!

September 15

It is enough to drive one mad, Wilhelm, to see people without any sense or feeling for the few remaining precious things in this world. You know of the walnut trees, where I sat with the good pastor of St. —— and Lotte—those noble walnut trees which, God knows, always filled me with a deep sense of joy! How friendly and cool they made the parsonage yard! How beautiful the branches were—and then the recollection of the good clergymen who had planted them so many years ago. The schoolmaster frequently mentioned the name of one of these, heard from his grandfather; he is said to have been such a good man, and his memory was ever sacred to me as I sat under the trees. I tell you, I saw tears in the schoolmaster's eyes when he spoke yesterday of their having been cut down. Cut down! I am furious and could kill the dog who struck the first blow with his ax. I would become utterly despondent if I should see only one such tree, standing in my courtyard, wither with age. Dearest friend, there is at least one redeeming feature in the situation. What a wonderful thing is human sympathy! The whole village grumbles; and I hope that the present pastor's wife will notice, in regard to butter, eggs, and other presents, how much she has hurt the feelings of the whole place. For it is *she,* the wife of the new pastor (our old one is dead), a thin and sickly creature who has every reason not to take any interest in the world, as no one takes any interest in her: a foolish woman who pretends to erudition, pokes her nose into an examination of the Canon, works a good deal at the new-fangled critico-moralist reformation of Christianity, and shrugs her shoulders at the excessive enthusiasm of Lavater. Her health is completely shattered, and for this reason she cannot find any pleasure in anything on God's earth. Only that sort of a creature could think of cutting down my walnut trees. You see, I cannot get over the shock! Just imagine, the falling leaves made her yard damp and dirty; the trees deprived her of sunlight; when the nuts were ripe, the boys pelted them with stones, and this made her nervous, this disturbed her profound meditations when she was weighing the merits of the differing arguments of Kennicot, Semler and Michaelis. When I saw how glum the villagers were, especially the old ones, I asked, "Why did you let it happen?" — "When the magistrate wants it," they answered, "what can you do?" But justice has triumphed. The magistrate, and the pastor (who, after all, wanted to profit from his wife's whims which anyway did not flavor his soup), had thought of sharing the proceeds; but the Board of Revenue still had old claims to the ground where the trees had stood; and the Board sold them to the highest bidder. There they lie! Oh, if I were a prince! I would know what to do—with the pastor's wife, the magistrate, and the Board of Revenue! —Prince! Indeed, if I were a prince, would I really worry about the trees of my country?

October 10

If I only see her dark eyes, I feel happy! But it makes me angry that Albert does not seem as delighted as he—hoped— as I—thought to be, if— I am not fond of dashes, but it is the only way of expressing myself here—and I think I make myself sufficiently clear.

Ossian has taken the place of Homer in my heart. What a world this sublime poet has opened to me! I wander with him over the heath, where the gale howls on all sides and sweeps along with it the spirits of our ancestors in the flowing mist and in the darkling light of the moon. I hear from the mountains, and in the roar of the torrent the faint groan of spirits in their caverns, and the lament of the maiden who pines for death beside the four moss-covered and grass-grown stones that mark the grave of her fallen hero, her lover. I then come upon the wandering gray bard who searches for the footsteps of his fathers on the vast heath and finds alas! only their tombstones; and then laments as he gazes at the lovely evening star reflected in the rolling waves of the sea. And I see past ages glow into life in the soul of the hero, when the friendly beam shone on the adventures of the brave, and the moonlight illuminated their ships, homeward bound and hung with wreaths of victory. When I read deep sorrow on the bard's brow, and see the last and lonely great one stagger exhausted toward his grave, drinking in ever-fresh, agonizing joys among the helpless shades of his dead companions, and then look down upon the cold earth and the tall waving grass, crying out: "The traveler will come, will come, who knew me in my beauty, and he will ask: 'Where is the bard, Fingal's great son?' His footsteps tread on my grave, and he will seek for me on this earth in vain." —O friend! I wish I could draw my sword like a noble paladin, and free my lord from the stabbing agony of a slowly ebbing life with one stroke; and then let my soul follow the liberated demigod.

October 19

Oh, this void, this terrifying void I feel in my breast! I often think: if you could once, only once, press her to your heart, this void would be filled.

October 26

Yes, dear friend, I feel more and more certain that the existence of any human being matters little, very little. A friend had come to visit Lotte, and I went into the next room and opened a book but could not read; then I took up a pen to write. I heard them speaking in low voices; they talked of unimportant matters and exchanged news of the town: how this girl would marry, how another was very ill. "She has a dry cough; the bones show in her face, and she has fainting spells; I wouldn't give a penny for her life," said the friend. "N.N. is also in very poor health," said Lotte. —"He is badly swollen," said the other. And my lively imagination carried me to the bedside of these unfortunates; I saw them reluctantly turning their backs on life while my little ladies, Wilhelm, talked as one talks about a stranger who is dying. And when I look around the room and see on all sides Lotte's dresses and Albert's papers, and the furniture, everything so familiar to me, even this inkwell, I think to myself: "See what you mean to this house! On the whole your friends respect you; you often make them happy, and it seems to your heart that it could not live without them; and yet—if you should go, if you should leave this circle, would they—how long would they feel the void which your loss will create in their destinies? how long?"—Oh, how transitory is man, that even in the place where he finds real confirmation of his existence, where he makes the one true impress of his personality in the memories, in the souls of those he loves, that even there he must fade and vanish, and how soon!

October 27

I often feel like tearing open my breast or knocking out my brains when I think how little human beings can do for one another. Oh, the love, the joy, the warmth and the delight which I do not feel myself, no other person will give me; and, with a heart full of supreme happiness, I still cannot make another person happy who stands before me cold and impassive.

October 27, evening.

I have so much in me, and the feeling for her absorbs it all; I have so much, and without her it all comes to nothing.

October 30

How many times have I been on the point of embracing her! God knows what a torture it is to see such loveliness moving about, and not to be permitted to stretch out one's hands to it; for this gesture is, after all, one of the most natural of human impulses. Do not children grasp at anything that comes their way?—And I?

November 3

I often lie down to sleep wishing—yes, sometimes hoping not to wake up again; and the next morning I open my eyes, again see the sun, and feel wretched. Oh, if I only could have moods, could shift the blame on the weather, a third person, or on an unsuccessful enterprise, then only half the weight of this unbearable burden of discontent would rest on me. Miserable me! I know only too well that the fault is with me alone—not fault! Enough, the source of all my misery is hidden in myself, as was formerly the source of all my happiness. Am I not the same who not long ago was intoxicated by the abundance of his emotions, and who stepped into a paradise wherever he went, with a heart ready longingly to embrace the whole world? And now this heart is dead, and thrills of delight radiate from it no longer; my eyes are dry, and my feelings, no longer refreshed by the relief of tears, contract my brow into anxious furrows. I suffer terribly because I have lost what was the one delight of my life—the holy, animating power that helped me to create worlds around me—it has gone! When I now look out of my window at the distant hill, and see how the early sun pierces the mist above it and lights up the peaceful meadows, and how the gentle river between its leafless willows winds toward me —oh, when this glorious Nature lies before me as immobile as on a little lacquered painting, and all this beauty cannot pump one single drop of happiness from my heart to my brain, and the whole man stands before the face of God like a dried-up well, like a broken pitcher—I have often thrown myself on the ground and implored God for tears, as a farmer prays for rain when the sky is leaden above him, and the ground around him is parched.

But alas! I feel that God does not send rain or sunshine because of our impetuous prayers; and those times that so torment me when I look back—why were they so blessed? Only because I patiently waited for His spirit, and embraced the joy that descended on me with an undivided, deeply grateful heart.

November 8

She has reproached me with my excesses! Oh, with what sweetness! My excesses: that now and then, when I allow myself a glass of wine, I drink the whole bottle. "Don't do it," she said. "Think of Lotte." — "Think!" I said, "do you need to tell me that? I think or I do not think. You are always before my soul. Today I sat near the place where you got out of the carriage the other day—" She began to speak of other matters, to keep me from pursuing that subject too deeply. Dear friend, I am lost! She can do with me as she wishes.

November 15

Thank you, Wilhelm, for your warm sympathy and your well-meaning advice; and, please, do not worry. Let me suffer to the end; in spite of my listlessness I still have enough strength to see it through. I have a deep respect for religion, you know that; I feel that it is a support for many weary souls, a comfort for many who die of thirst. Only—can it, must it, be that for everyone? When you look at the great world, you see thousands for whom it has meant nothing, thousands for whom it will never mean anything, preached or not preached; and must it then mean something to me? Did not even the Son of God say that those would be about Him whom His Father had given Him? What if I should not have been given to Him? Suppose, as my heart tells me, God the Father wanted to keep me for Himself? — Please, do not interpret this wrongly; do not see any sarcasm in these innocent words; it is my whole soul which I lay open to you; otherwise I should prefer to have kept silence; for, as you know, I do not like to waste words concerning matters of which everyone else is as ignorant as myself. Is it not man's destiny to bear his lot patiently and to drain the cup to the dregs? Yet did not the cup become too bitter for the human lips of God's only Son? Why, then, should I brag and pretend that it tastes sweet to me? And why should I be ashamed at the terrible moment when my whole life trembles between being and not-being; when the past flashes like lightning over the gloomy abyss of the future and everything around me collapses, and the world is destroyed with me—is it not then the voice of a creature thrown completely on his own resources, who has failed himself and is resistlessly plunging into the abyss, that grinds out the cry, "My God! My God! why hast Thou forsaken me?" And should I be ashamed to use those words; should I fear the moment not spared Him who rolls the heavens together like a scroll?

November 21

She does not see, she does not realize, that she is preparing a poison that will be the ruin of us both; and I voluptuously drain the cup she hands me for my destruction. What is the meaning of the friendly glance she often—often?—no, not often but still, at times, gives me, of the pleasure with which she accepts an involuntary expression of my emotion, of the compassion for my suffering which appears on her brow?

Yesterday, when I was leaving, she gave me her hand and said: "Adieu, dear Werther!" —Dear Werther! It was the first time she had called me "dear," and the word went to the marrow of my bones. I have repeated it to myself a hundred times; and last night, before I went to bed, I talked all sorts of nonsense. I suddenly said, "Good night, dear Werther!" and afterward had to laugh at myself.

November 22

I cannot pray, "Let her be mine!" And yet how often do I think of her as mine. I cannot pray, "Give her to me!" because she belongs to another man. I go on joking at my suffering, and if I gave myself up to this game, it would bring on a whole litany of antitheses.

She feels how I am suffering. Today her glance went straight to my heart. I found her alone; I did not speak and she looked at me. And I no longer saw her lovable beauty, no longer the gentle light of her exquisite spirit; all that disappeared. I saw a far more wonderful look in her eyes: an expression of warmest sympathy, of the sweetest compassion. Why was I not allowed to throw myself at her feet? Why could I not take her in my arms and answer her with a thousand kisses? She took refuge at the clavichord, and her soft voice breathed out a melody to the accompaniment of her playing. Never have I seen her lips so charming; it was as if they opened thirstily, to drink in the sweet tones which welled up from the instrument; as if only a mysterious echo reverberated from her innocent mouth. If I could only describe it to you! I was resigned; I bowed my head and vowed: "Never shall I dare to kiss those lips, on which heavenly spirits hover." And yet—I shall— Ha! you see, it stands like a barrier before my soul—this supreme happiness —and then die to atone for my sin—sin?

November 26

Sometimes I say to myself: "Your destiny is unique; call the others fortunate—no one has been so tormented as you." Then I read an ancient poet, and it seems to me as though I look into my own heart. I have so much to endure! Oh, were there other men before me as miserable as I?

November 30

I cannot, I cannot regain my balance! Wherever I go I am faced with an apparition which completely upsets me. Today! O Destiny! O Mankind!

I was walking by the river at noon; I had no desire to eat. Everything was bleak; a cold and humid westerly wind blew from the mountains, and the gray rain clouds drifted into the valley. Some distance away I saw a man in a shabby green coat crawling among the rocks and evidently looking for herbs. When I came closer and the noise I made caused him to turn, I saw a very interesting face, whose main feature was a quiet melancholy and which otherwise expressed nothing but a frank good-natured disposition. Part of his long black hair was fastened into two rolls with pins, and the rest, braided into a thick queue, hung down his back. As his clothes indicated a man of the lower classes, I thought he would not resent my interest in what he was doing; so I asked him what he was looking for. "I am looking for flowers," he answered with a deep sigh, "but I do not find any." — "This is not the right season of the year," I said, smiling. — "There are so many flowers," he said, coming down toward me. "In my garden are roses and honeysuckle of two kinds, one of which my father gave me; they grow like weeds; I have already looked for two days for them and cannot find them. There are always flowers out here, too, yellow and blue and red ones; and the thousand-guilder-plant has a lovely little flower. I cannot find any at all." I noticed something queer about him and therefore asked cautiously, "What will you do with the flowers?" A strange convulsive smile flashed over his face. "If you won't betray me," he said, pressing a finger on his mouth, "I have promised my sweetheart a nosegay." — "That is very nice of you," I said. — "Oh," he said, "she has a lot of other things; she is rich." — "And yet she will like your nosegay," I said. — "Oh," he rambled on, "she has jewels and a crown." — "What is her name?" — "If the States-General would only pay me," he replied, "I would be a different person! Yes, there was a time when I was well off. Now I am done for. Now I am—" A tearful look heavenward expressed everything. "So you were happy?" I asked. — "Oh, I wish I were so again!" he answered. "I felt as fine, as gay, as light as a fish in the water." — "Heinrich!" an old woman who came toward us called. "Heinrich, where are you? We have looked everywhere for you. Come and eat." — "Is he your son?" I asked, going up to her. — "Yes, my poor son!" she replied. "God has put a heavy cross on my shoulders." — "How long has he been like this?" I asked. — "He has been quiet now for six months," she said. "Thank God he has improved; before then he was raving mad for a whole year and lay in chains in the madhouse. Now he wouldn't do harm to anyone, and he talks of nothing but kings and emperors. He was such a good-natured, quiet boy, who helped support me, and wrote a beautiful hand, and all of a sudden he became gloomy, fell into a violent fever, then into stark madness, and he is now as you see him. If I could tell you, sir—" I interrupted the flow of her words with the question, "What did he mean when he spoke of a time when he was so happy and well off?" — "The foolish fellow!" she cried, with a compassionate smile, "by that he means the time when he was out of his mind; he always praises those days; it was when he was at the asylum and did not know himself." The last expression struck me like a thunderbolt; I pressed some money into her hand and left her in haste.

"When you were happy!" I cried aloud, while I hurried back to the town, "when you felt as carefree as a fish in the water. God in Heaven! did you make it men's destiny only to be happy before they come to reason and after they have lost it again? Poor fellow!—and yet how I envy you your melancholy mind and the confusion of your senses in which you wander. Full of hope, you set out to pick flowers for your queen—in winter—and you are sad because you do not find any and do not understand why you cannot find any. And

I—I set out without hope, without a purpose, and return home just as I came. You imagine what a person you would be if the States-General would pay you. Happy creature, who can blame an earthly impediment for his lack of happiness. You do not feel! You do not know that your misery lies in your ruined heart, in your ruined brain, and that all the kings and emperors of this world cannot help you."

He should perish without comfort who mocks at a sick man for traveling to the remotest medicinal springs, even though these may only increase his sickness and make his final exit more painful! who feels superior to the oppressed heart that sets forth on a pilgrimage to the Holy Sepulcher to free itself from pangs of conscience and sufferings of the soul. Every footstep on an unbeaten path that bruises the feet is a drop of balm for an anguished spirit, and, at the end of a day's journey thus endured, that heart will lie down to rest, eased of many a sorrow. And can you call all this delusion, you armchair quibblers? Delusion! O God, you see my tears! Did You, who created man so poor, have to give him fellow creatures who deprive him of his little poverty, of his little confidence in You, You All-loving Father! For what is trust in a healing root, in the tears of the vine—what is it but trust in You, that You have endowed everything that surrounds us with the power of healing and soothing which we need every hour? Father, whom I do not know! Father, who once filled my whole soul and has now turned His face from me! Call me to You! Break Your silence! Your silence will not keep this soul from thirsting. And is it possible that a

human father could be angry when his unexpectedly returning son embraces him, crying: "I am back again, Father.
Don't be angry that I interrupted my journey, which you
wanted me to continue. The world is everywhere the same—
trouble and work, reward and pleasure; but what is that to
me? I am only happy where you are, and I want to suffer
and to enjoy in your presence." —And You, dear Heavenly
Father, would You turn him away from You?

December 1

Wilhelm! the man I wrote you about, the happy unfortunate
man, was a clerk in Lotte's father's office; and a desperate
passion for her, which he fostered, concealed, confessed, and
which finally cost him his position, has driven him mad. Try
to imagine from these dry words how this story upset me
when Albert told it as calmly as you will, perhaps, read it.

December 4

I beg you—you see, I am done for; I cannot bear it any
longer. Today I sat near her as she played the clavichord, all
sorts of tunes and with so much expression. So much! So
much! What could I do? Her little sister sat on my knee and

dressed her doll. Tears came into my eyes. I bowed my head and caught sight of her wedding ring. The tears ran down my cheeks—and suddenly Lotte began to play the heavenly old melody. All at once my soul was touched by a feeling of consolation, by a memory of the past, of the other occasions when I had heard the song, of the dark intervals of vexation between, of shattered hopes, and then—I walked up and down the room, my heart almost suffocated by the rush of emotions. "For God's sake," I said, in a vehement outburst, "for God's sake, stop!" She paused and looked at me steadily. "Werther," she said with a smile that went deep to my heart, "Werther, you are very sick. You dislike the things you once liked. Go! I beg you, calm yourself!" I tore myself from her sight, and—God! you see my misery and will put an end to it.

December 6

How her image haunts me! Awake or asleep, she fills my entire being. Here, when I close my eyes, here, in my forehead, at the focus of my inner vision, her dark eyes remain. Here! but I cannot put it into words. When I close my eyes, they are there; like an ocean, like an abyss, they lie before me, in me, taking hold of all my thoughts.

What is man, that celebrated demigod! Does he not lack powers just where he needs them most? And when he soars with joy, or sinks into suffering, is he not in both cases held back and restored to dull, cold consciousness at the very moment when he longs to lose himself in the fullness of the Infinite?

[THE EDITOR TO THE READER]

I should very much prefer that documents written in his own hand concerning the last remarkable days of our friend were at our disposal, and that it were not necessary for me to interrupt the sequence of his posthumous letters by direct narration.

I have taken great pains to collect exact facts by word of mouth from those who were well informed about his history; it is a simple story, and, apart from a few details, all evidence agrees. It is only with regard to the emotional attitude of the actors that opinions differ and judgment is divided.

Nothing remains for us but to relate conscientiously what we were able to gather after repeated efforts, to insert the letters found after our friend's death and to consider the smallest note valuable, for the particular reason that it is so difficult to uncover the true and real motives of even a single action by persons who are not of the usual type.

Depression and apathy had more and more rooted themselves in Werther's mind, had become tangled and gradually had taken hold of his whole being. The harmony of his spirit was totally destroyed; an inner heat and vehemence, unsettling all the forces of his nature, produced the most adverse effects and left him finally in an exhausted condition, out of which he struggled more desperately than when fighting against former troubles. The anguish of his heart consumed his spirit's remaining powers, his vivacity, and his bright intellect. He became a depressing companion, more and more unhappy and more unjust due to this unhappiness. So, at least, say Albert's friends; they maintain that Werther had been unable to judge a simple, quiet man to whom had been given a long-wished-for happiness which he hoped to preserve for the years to come, Werther himself being a person who squandered, as it were, every day all he had, and then suffered and was in need in the evening. Albert, they said, had not changed in so short a time; he was still the same person whom Werther had known, had respected and admired from the beginning of their acquaintance. Albert loved Lotte above everything; he was proud of her and wished that everyone recognize her as a woman above women. Can anyone, therefore, blame him for wishing to avoid even the shadow of suspicion, for not being inclined to share this treasure even in the most harmless way? His friends do not deny that Albert frequently left the room when Werther was with Lotte; but this was neither because of hate nor because of antipathy toward his friend, but only because of his feeling that Werther was depressed by his presence.

Lotte's father felt indisposed and could not leave the

house. Therefore, he sent his carriage for her, and she drove out to see him. It was a lovely winter day; the first snow had fallen heavily and covered the whole countryside.

The next morning Werther went out to join her and, if Albert could not come, to accompany her home.

The clear weather had no effect on his gloomy mood; a dull weight pressed on his soul; the sad scenes he had recently witnessed were branded in his memory; and nothing but one painful thought after another crossed his brooding mind. Since he was in constant struggle with himself, the circumstances of others, too, seemed to him precarious and confused. He believed that he had destroyed the harmonious relationship between Albert and his wife, and he reproached himself, at the same time, that he mixed with this reproach a secret indignation against the husband.

His thoughts revolved the same questions while he walked along. "Yes, yes," he said to himself, grinding his teeth, "so that is companionship—intimate, friendly, affectionate, sympathetic—a placid and constant loyalty! It is, as a matter of fact, satiety and indifference! Doesn't he take more interest in any trifling piece of business than in his dear, delightful wife? Does he appreciate his good fortune? Does he know how to respect her as she deserves? He has her—very well—he has her—I know that, as I know some other things too. I thought I had become used to it, but it is going to drive me mad; it is going to kill me. And has his friendship stood the test? Does he not already see in my devotion to Lotte a trespassing on his own rights, and in my attentions to her a mute reproach? I know well. I feel that he does not like my coming to the house; he wishes me away and cannot bear my presence."

Werther often slowed his brisk pace and often, stopping short, seemed to consider going back; but again and again he directed his steps forward and, engaged in these thoughts and soliloquies, and almost against his will, eventually arrived at the hunting lodge.

He went into the house, asking for Lotte and her father, and found the whole family rather upset. The oldest boy told him that a calamity had occurred in Wahlheim; a peasant had been murdered. This piece of news did not make any special impression on Werther. —He entered the room and found Lotte trying to persuade her father not to go to Wahlheim, as he intended to do, in spite of his illness, in order to hold an inquest on the scene of the deed. The identity of the murderer was still unknown; the murdered man had been found that morning in front of his house. There was some suspicion: the victim had been employed by a widow who formerly had another man in her service, and this former servant had left her house after some altercation.

When Werther heard this, he became very excited. "Is it possible!" he exclaimed, "I must go there at once; I could not have a quiet moment otherwise." He rushed to Wahlheim, living over in his mind all he knew of the matter; he did not for one moment doubt that the murder had been committed by the man with whom he had so often talked and who had become so important to him. As Werther crossed under the linden trees to reach the inn where they had brought the dead man, he shuddered at the sight of this formerly beloved place. The threshold, where the children of the neighbors had so often played, was spattered with blood. Love and loyalty, the most beautiful of human emotions, had turned into violence and murder. The great trees were without foliage and rimmed with hoarfrost; the lovely hedges which arched over the low wall of the churchyard were bare; and the snow-covered gravestones could be seen through the gaps.

When he came nearer to the inn, in front of which the whole village had gathered, shouts were suddenly heard. A group of armed men could be seen in the distance, and everyone cried out that the murderer had been arrested. Werther looked in that direction and was no longer in doubt. Yes! it was the young farm hand who had loved the widow so ardently, and whom he had met not long ago roaming about in a state of suppressed rage and silent despair.

"What have you done, you unfortunate fellow!" exclaimed Werther, going up to the prisoner. The young man looked at him quietly and in silence, but said at last, with great calm: "No one is going to have her; she will have no one!" They took the prisoner into the inn, and Werther left in haste. The horrible and violent meeting had shaken him through and through. For one short moment he had been torn from his melancholy, his gloom and his apathetic resignation; he was overcome by compassion and moved by an irresistible desire to save this man, whose predicament he felt deeply. He considered him, even as a criminal, to be free of real guilt, and identified himself so completely with him that he was certain to be able to also convince others. He could not wait to plead for him; the most persuasive arguments rose to his lips; he walked quickly back to the hunting lodge and could not keep himself from rehearsing, in an undertone, as he went along, the defense he wanted to present to the bailiff.

When he entered the house, he found that Albert had arrived; this dampened his spirits for a moment but he managed, after a while, to control himself and began to impress his opinions on the bailiff with much warmth. The latter shook his head repeatedly, and although Werther with the greatest brilliance, passion and truth put forward everything a human being could say to exculpate another human being, the bailiff remained unmoved, as one can easily understand. He did not even allow our friend to finish his discourse but eagerly contradicted him and reproached him for defending an assassin. He pointed out to him that in this way every law would be annulled, the whole security of the state endangered; and besides, he added, he himself would not be able to do anything in a case like this without taking upon himself the heaviest responsibility. Everything would have to be done in the legal way, and according to instructions.

Werther did not yet surrender, and implored the bailiff to look the other way if someone tried to help the man escape. This, too, the bailiff refused to do. Albert, who had finally joined in the discussion, sided with the older man. Werther was overruled and left in a terrible state of suffering after the bailiff had said to him several times: "No, there is no help for him."

How deeply these words must have struck him we can see from a note found among his papers, undoubtedly written that same day.

"There is no help for you, unfortunate man! I see only too well that there is no help for us!"

Albert's final words in the matter of the prisoner, spoken in the bailiff's presence, had disgusted Werther extremely: he thought he noticed in them a slight irritability toward himself. And though, on further reflection, he could not fail to see that both men were probably right, he still felt that he would sacrifice his integrity if he should confess, if he should admit that it was so. A note related to this conflict, which perhaps expresses his whole relation to Albert, has been found among his papers.

"What is the use of my saying to myself again and again: He is honest and good; but it still breaks my heart; I cannot be just."

As the evening was mild and the snow had begun to melt, Lotte and Albert walked home. On the way Lotte now and then looked back, as though she missed Werther's company. Albert began to speak of Werther; he criticized him, although he did him full justice. He touched upon his unfortunate passion and expressed the wish that it might be possible to send him away. "I wish this for your sake, as well," he said; "and," he added, "I implore you to try and turn his attentions to you in another direction and limit his frequent visits, which have already been generally noticed and have caused a certain amount of talk." Lotte was silent, and Albert seems to have resented her silence, since from that time on he did not mention Werther again, and, whenever she spoke of him, stopped the conversation or changed the subject.

Werther's unsuccessful attempt to help the unfortunate man was the last flare of a fading light; after this he sank only deeper into his grief and apathy and became almost frantic when he heard that he might be called to testify against the man, who had, by now, taken to denying everything.

All the unpleasantnesses that he had ever faced during his official life, the humiliation at the Count's party, as well as every other situation in which he had failed, now came and went in his mind. Somehow he found in all this a justification for his present inactivity; he felt himself cut off from any prospects, incapable of grasping any of those chances by which one takes hold of the occupations of everyday life; and, completely absorbed in his curious emotional state, his way of thinking and his hopeless passion, in the unchanging monotony of a cheerless relationship with the lovable and beloved creature whose peace he disturbed, straining his powers to the utmost but wearing them out without purpose and prospect—he steadily advanced toward his tragic end.

A few posthumous letters are the most convincing evidence of his confused state of mind, of his passion, of his restless actions and efforts, and of his weariness of life; and we are therefore inserting them here.

"December 12

"Dear Wilhelm, my condition is one which those unfortunate people who were thought to be hunted by evil spirits must have experienced. I am sometimes gripped by something that is neither anxiety nor desire; it is an unfamiliar inner rage which threatens to tear open my breast, which clutches at my throat. Oh, it hurts, it hurts! And then I wander about in the dreadful night scenes of this inhuman time of year.

"Last night something drove me out of the house. A thaw had suddenly set in, and I had heard that the river had overflowed and all the brooks were swollen, and that my dear valley, in its whole length, from Wahlheim down, was flooded. After eleven at night I hurried out. It was terrifying to see from the rock the churning waters whirling in the moonlight, gushing forth over meadows, fields, and hedges; and up and down the broad valley one tempestuous sea under the howling wind! And when the moon came out again and rested on a black cloud, and the flood rolled and roared before me in the terrible, magnificent light, I shuddered with awe and also with longing. Oh, with wide-open arms I faced the abyss and breathed: 'Down, down!' and was lost in an ecstatic wish to hurl down all my agonies, all my sufferings! to storm along with the waves! Yet I did not have the strength to lift my feet from the ground and end all my agony. —My hourglass has not yet run out, I feel it! Oh, Wilhelm, how gladly would I have surrendered my mortal existence, to tear the clouds apart with that gale and to embrace the floods. Ha! will not the prisoner some day be granted this bliss? —And when I looked down with nostalgic longing at the spot where I had once rested with Lotte, under a willow, after a long walk in the summer's heat, I saw that it was also flooded; I could hardly make out where the willow stood. Wilhelm! And I thought of her meadows, of the whole countryside around the hunting lodge, of our arbor, now shattered by the raving torrent. And a sun shaft of the past pierced through, as when a prisoner has a vision of flocks and herds, meadows and former dignities. I remained standing there! I do not blame myself, for I have the courage to die. I should have— Now I am sitting here like an old woman who gleans her firewood from the fences and begs her bread from door to door, so as to prolong and to ease her wasting and cheerless existence for another short space of time."

"*December 14*

"What is this, what has happened to me, dear friend? I am alarmed at myself. Is not my love for her the most sacred, the purest, the most brotherly love? Have I ever felt any culpable desire in my soul? But I will not protest! —And now—dreams! Oh, how right were the instincts of those peoples who attributed such contradictory effects to unknown powers! Last night—I tremble to confess it—I held her in my arms, close to my breast, and covered her love-murmuring lips with endless kisses; my eyes sank into the intoxication of hers. Dear God! Am I culpable that I even now feel a supreme happiness in again living through those glowing moments of joy in all their intensity? Lotte! Lotte! —And this is the end! My mind is in a daze; for a week I have not been able to concentrate, my eyes are full of tears. I feel nowhere at home, and everywhere at home. I have no wish; I make no demand. It would be better for me to leave."

It was about this time, and under these circumstances, that Werther gradually became confirmed in his resolution to leave this world. Since his return to Lotte, this resolution had been always his last straw, his last hope; but he had made up his mind that it should result in no headlong or rash act; that he would take this step with full premeditation and with the coolest possible determination.

His doubts, and his inner struggle are evident from a note which was probably the beginning of a letter to Wilhelm and was found, without date, among his papers:

"Her presence, her destiny, and her sympathy with mine press the last tears from my ebbing mind.

"To lift the curtain and step behind it! That is all! And

why with fear and trembling? Because no one knows what one may see there? or because one cannot return? Or because it is, after all, a peculiarity of our mind to apprehend that confusion and darkness exist in places of which we know nothing definite?"

Finally the tragic thought became more and more familiar to him, and his plan became firm and irrevocable, as witness the following ambiguous letter written to his friend.

"December 20

"I owe it to your love, Wilhelm, that you understood my words as you did. Yes, you are right; it would be better for me to leave. Your suggestion that I return to you all does not quite satisfy me; at least I should like to come by a round-about way, especially as we can expect continued frost and good roads. I am very glad that you intend to come and fetch me; if you will only wait another two weeks until I have written you a second letter with further details. No fruit should be picked before it is ripe. And two weeks more or less make a great difference. Please tell my mother that she should pray for her son, who asks forgiveness for all the trouble he has given her. It was my destiny to hurt those to whom I owed happiness. Farewell, dearest friend! May Heaven bless you. Farewell!"

What happened at this time in Lotte's heart, how she felt about her husband and about her unhappy friend, we hardly dare express in words, though, knowing her character, we can form for ourselves a faint idea; and the sensitive soul of a woman will be able to enter into her thought and feelings.

So much is certain—that she had firmly decided by herself to do everything that would keep Werther at a distance and that her hesitation was based on a warm feeling of pity for her friend, as she knew how difficult, yes, how almost impossible, the separation would be for him. She felt, however, at this time, a still greater pressure in herself to act; her husband had become completely silent about this relationship, and, as she herself had never touched the subject again, she now wished all the more to give actual proof that her feelings toward Albert were worthy of his toward her.

On the same day that Werther wrote the letter to his friend which we have given above—it was the Sunday before Christmas—he came to see Lotte in the evening and found her alone. She was busy arranging some toys she had made for her younger sisters and brothers. Werther spoke of the pleasure the children would have and of the times when the unexpected opening of a door and the sight of a Christmas tree trimmed with wax candles and hung with candies and apples made one speechless with delight. "You also are going to get Christmas presents," said Lotte, hiding her embarrassment under a sweet smile, "if you are very good: a little roll of wax tapers and something more." — "And what do you call good?" he cried. "How shall I be? How can I be, dearest Lotte?" — "Thursday night is Christmas Eve," she said, "when the children will come here with my father, and everyone will receive his presents. Do come, too—but not before." Werther was taken aback. "Please," she continued, "that's how it is; I implore you, for the sake of my peace of mind. It cannot, cannot go on like this." He turned away and paced up and down the room, muttering to himself that phrase, "It cannot go on like this." Lotte, who sensed the terrible state of mind into which her words had thrown him, tried to divert his thoughts with all sorts of questions, but in vain. "No, Lotte," he exclaimed, "I shall not see you again!" —"Why not?" she asked. "Werther! You can, you must see us again; only do be reasonable. Oh, why did you have to be born with this violent temper, this uncontrollable clinging passion for everything you touch! Please," she said, taking his hand, "be reasonable! Your intellect, your knowledge, your talents, should offer you such a variety of satisfactions! Be a man! Get rid of this hopeless attachment to one who can do nothing but pity you." He gritted his teeth and gave her a dark look. She kept his hand in hers. "Think it over calmly, if only for a moment, Werther!" she said. "Do you not feel that you deceive yourself, that you deliberately ruin yourself? Why must it be I, Werther? Just I, who belong to another? Why must that be? I am afraid, very much afraid, that it is only the impossibility of possessing me that attracts you so much." —He withdrew his hand, giving her a fixed and angry look. "Clever!" he mocked, "very clever. Did Albert perhaps make that remark? Diplomatic, very diplomatic!" —"Anyone might make it," she retorted. "And should there exist in the wide world no other girl who could satisfy the desires of your heart? Take your courage in both hands and look for her—I swear you will find her. I have been worried for a long time, for you and for us, about your self-banishment to this narrow circle. Make up your mind! Travel will and must distract you! Look around and find an object worthy of your love; then come back and enjoy with us the pure happiness of true friendship."

"All that should be printed," he said with a frozen smile, "and we could recommend it to educators. Dear Lotte, give me a little time and everything will turn out well." —"Only one thing more, Werther, do not return before Christmas Eve!" He was about to answer when Albert entered. They exchanged a rather frigid "Good evening!" and walked up and down the room together in some embarrassment. Werther then began a conversation on unimportant matters, but it soon petered out. Albert did the same and then asked his wife about some errands he had wanted her to do for him. When he heard that they had not been done, he spoke some words to her which sounded to Werther cold and even harsh. Werther wanted to leave, but he did not have the power, and he delayed until eight o'clock. All this time he was becoming more and more irritated and angry; and, when the table was set, he took his hat and stick, although Albert invited him to stay for supper. Werther imagined this to be only a conventional gesture of politeness, thanked him coldly, and left.

He returned to his lodging, took the candle from the hand of his servant, who wanted to light him upstairs, and went alone to his room. There he burst into uncontrolled loud weeping, talked to himself in great agitation, pacing excitedly up and down, and finally flung himself on his bed, without taking off his clothes, where his servant found him when, plucking up courage, he went in about eleven o'clock to ask if his master wanted him to pull off his boots. Werther allowed him to do this but told him not to come into the room in the morning before he called.

On Monday morning, the twenty-first of December, he wrote the following letter to Lotte; it was found sealed on his writing desk after his death and was brought to her. I shall insert parts of it here at intervals, as it appears from later events that it was written in a fragmentary manner.

"It is decided, Lotte, that I shall die, and I am writing you this calmly, without any romantic exaltation, on the morning of the day when I shall see you for the last time. When you read this, my dearest, the cold grave will already cover the stiffened body of the restless, unfortunate man who does not know any sweeter way to pass the last moments of his life than to talk to you. I have had a terrible, but ah, what a wonderful night. It has strengthened and confirmed my resolution: to die! Yesterday, when I tore myself away from you, my whole nature in terrible revolt, everything rushing into my heart, and when my hopeless, cheerless existence so close to you overwhelmed me with a ghastly chill—I was hardly able to reach my room; almost beside myself, I fell on my knees, and, O God, you granted me a last consolation of bitter tears! A thousand plans, a thousand hopes raged in my soul, but finally it was there, firmly, wholly, the one last thought: to die! I lay down, and this morning, in the peace of awakening, it is still firm, still strong in my heart: to die! —It is not despair; it is the certainty that I have suffered enough, and that I am sacrificing myself for you. Yes, Lotte! Why should I hide it from you? One of us three must go, and I am to be that one! O my dearest, my wounded heart has been haunted by a terrible demon—often. To murder your husband! Or you! Or myself! Well, so be it! When you walk to the top of the mountain, on a fine summer evening, remember me; how I often came up there from the valley to meet you; and then look across to the churchyard and to my grave, where the wind gently sways the tall grass in the light of the setting sun. —I was calm when I began to write this letter and now, now I am weeping like a child, when all this comes so vividly to my mind."

Shortly before ten o'clock Werther called his servant and, while dressing, told him that, since he would leave this place in a few days, he should clean his clothes and prepare everything for packing. He also gave him the order to ask everywhere for any bills to his account, to collect some books which he had loaned, and to pay the poor people to whom he had usually given some money every week, a sum covering two months.

He had his dinner served in his room and afterward rode out to the bailiff's house but did not find him at home. Lost in thought, he walked up and down in the garden, evidently overwhelmed in his mind with all his sad memories in these last months.

The children did not long leave him in peace but followed him and ran up to him, saying that when tomorrow had come, and again tomorrow, and another day after that, they would go to Lotte's and get their Christmas presents; and they told him about the marvels which their childish imagination promised them. "Tomorrow," he cried, "and again tomorrow and still another day after that!" and kissed them all affectionately and was about to leave when the smallest boy tried to whisper something in his ear. He confided that his big brothers had written beautiful New Year's greetings, *so* big! one for Papa, one for Albert and Lotte, and one for Herr Werther, too! and that they would themselves deliver them early on New Year's Day. This almost broke Werther's heart. He gave something to each of the children, mounted his horse, sent his greetings to the old man, and rode away with tears in his eyes.

About five o'clock in the afternoon he arrived at his lodging and ordered the housemaid to see that the fire be kept burning until late that night. He told his servant to pack his books and his linen at the bottom of his trunk and to make a bundle of his clothes. It was probably then he wrote the following passage of his last letter to Lotte:

"You do not expect me! You think I shall obey you and not see you again until Christmas Eve. O Lotte! today or never again. On Christmas Eve you will hold this piece of paper in your hand, trembling and covering it with your sweet tears. I will, I must! Oh, how relieved I am now that I have made up my mind."

Meanwhile, Lotte was in a peculiar frame of mind. After her last talk with Werther she had realized how hard it would be for her to be separated from him, and how he would suffer if he had to leave her.

She had mentioned almost casually in Albert's presence that Werther would not return until Christmas Eve; and Albert had ridden out to see an official in the neighborhood with whom he had to settle some business, and where he would have to spend the night.

Now she sat at home alone—none of her family was with her—and she gave herself up to her thoughts, which quietly moved over her circumstances. She saw herself united forever to the husband whose love and loyalty she knew, to whom she was deeply devoted and whose calmness of disposition and whose trustworthiness seemed to be intended by Providence for a good wife to build on it her life's happiness; she keenly realized how much he would always mean to her and to her children. On the other hand, Werther had become very dear to her heart; from the very beginning of their acquaintance the harmony of their minds had showed itself in the most pleasant way, and continued friendly relations with him as well as their many mutual experiences had made a lasting impression on her heart. She had become accustomed to share with him everything of interest she felt or thought; and his departure threatened to create a great gap in her existence which could not be filled again. Oh, if she only had the power to transform him this very moment into a brother, how happy she would be!—had she only been fortunate enough to marry him off to one of her friends, or could she be allowed to hope that his friendship with Albert might be completely restored!

She passed all her friends in review, one after the other, but found a flaw in each and could not think of one girl to whom she would not have begrudged Werther.

As she pondered on all this, she felt for the first time, keenly if subconsciously, that in her heart of hearts she secretly wished to keep him for herself, at the same time saying to herself that she could not, should not, keep him; her innocent, noble nature, usually so light and resourceful, felt the weight of a melancholy that sees all hope for happiness barred. Her heart was oppressed, and a dark mist lay upon her eyes.

It was half past six when she heard Werther coming up the stairs; she immediately recognized his step, and his voice as he asked for her. Her heart beat violently, we may say almost for the first time, at his arrival. She would have preferred to have had him told she was not at home; and when he came into the room, she received him in a kind of frantic

confusion with the words, "You have broken your promise!"
—"I did not promise anything," was his answer. —"But you
could at least have respected my request," she said. "I asked
you not to come, for my peace and yours!"

She did not quite know what she did or said as she sent a
message to some friends because she did not wish to be alone
with Werther. He had brought her some books and asked
her about others while she wished, now, that her friends
would arrive, now, that they would not. The maid returned,
bringing a message that both girls were unable to come.

At first she thought of having her maid sit with her work
in the adjoining room, but she then changed her mind. Werther paced up and down the room, and she went to the clavichord and began to play a minuet; but it did not go
smoothly. She recovered herself and sat down quietly beside
Werther, who had taken his customary place on the sofa.

"Don't you have anything to read to me?" she asked. He
had nothing. "In my drawer over there," she began, "is your
translation of some of the songs of Ossian. I have not yet read
them because I always hoped you would read them to me.
But lately there has never been any time or occasion." He
smiled and took out the songs; a shudder ran through him as
he took them in his hands, and his eyes filled with tears as he
looked at the written pages. He sat down again and read:

"Star of descending night! fair is thy light in the west!
Thou liftest thy unshorn head from thy cloud; thy steps are
stately on thy hill. What dost thou behold in the plain? The

stormy winds are laid. The murmur of the torrent comes from afar. Roaring waves climb the distant rock. The flies of evening are on their feeble wings; the hum of their course is on the field. What dost thou behold, fair light? But thou dost smile and depart. The waves come with joy around thee; they bathe thy lovely hair. Farewell, thou silent beam! Let the light of Ossian's soul arise!

"And it does arise in its strength! I behold my departed friends. Their gathering is on Lora, as in the days of other years. Fingal comes like a watery column of mist; his heroes are around, and, see! the bards of song—gray-haired Ullin! stately Ryno! Alpin, with the tuneful voice! the soft complaint of Minona! How are you changed, my friends, since the days of Selma's feast, when we contended, like gales of spring as they fly along the hill, and bend by turns the feebly whistling grass.

"Minona came forth in her beauty, with downcast look and tearful eye. Her hair flew slowly on the blast that rushed unfrequent from the hill. The souls of the heroes were sad when she raised the tuneful voice. Often had they seen the grave of Salgar, the dark dwelling of white-bosomed Colma. Colma left alone on the hill, with all her voice of song! Salgar promised to come; but the night descended around. Hear the voice of Colma, when she sat alone on the hill!

"COLMA: It is night; I am alone, forlorn on the hill of storms. The wind is heard on the mountain. The torrent is howling down the rock. No hut receives me from the rain; forlorn on the hill of winds!

"Rise, moon, from behind thy clouds! Stars of the night, arise! Lead me, some light, to the place where my love rests from the chase alone! His bow near him unstrung, his dogs panting around him! But here I must sit alone by the rock of the mossy stream. The stream and the wind roar aloud. I hear not the voice of my love! Why delays my Salgar; why the chief of the hill his promise? Here is the rock, and here the tree; here is the roaring stream! Thou didst promise with night to be here. Ah, whither is my Salgar gone? With thee I would fly from my father, with thee from my brother of pride. Our race have long been foes: we are not foes, O Salgar!

"Cease a little while, O wind! stream, be thou silent awhile! Let my voice be heard around; let my wanderer hear me! Salgar! it is Colma who calls. Here is the tree and the rock. Salgar, my love, I am here! Why delayest thou thy coming? Lo! the calm moon comes forth. The flood is bright in the vale; the rocks are gray on the steep. I see him not on the brow. His dogs come not before him with tidings of his near approach. Here I must sit alone!

"Who lie on the heath beside me? Are they my love and my brother? Speak to me, O my friends! To Colma they give no reply. Speak to me: I am alone! My soul is tormented with fears. Ah, they are dead! Their swords are red from the fight. Oh, my brother! my brother! why hast thou slain my Salgar? Why, O Salgar! hast thou slain my brother? Dear were ye both to me! what shall I say in your praise? Thou wert fair on the hill among thousands! he was terrible in fight! Speak to me! hear my voice! hear me, sons of my love! They are silent, silent forever! Cold, cold are their breasts of clay! Oh, from the rock on the hill, from the top of the windy steep, speak ye ghosts of the dead! Speak, I will not be afraid! Whither are ye gone to rest? In what cave of the hill shall I find the departed? No feeble voice is on the gale: no answer half drowned in the storm!

"I sit in my grief: I wait for morning in my tears! Rear the tomb, ye friends of the dead. Close it not till Colma comes. My life flies away like a dream. Why should I stay behind? Here shall I rest with my friends, by the stream of the sounding rock. When night comes on the hill—when the loud winds arise, my ghost shall stand in the blast, and mourn the death of my friends. The hunter shall hear from his booth; he shall fear, but love my voice! For sweet shall my voice be for my friends: pleasant were her friends to Colma.

"Such was thy song, Minona, softly blushing daughter of Torman. Our tears descended for Colma, and our souls were sad! Ullin came with his harp; he gave the song of Alpin. The voice of Alpin was pleasant; the soul of Ryno was a beam of fire! But they had rested in the narrow house; their voice had ceased in Selma! Ullin had returned one day from the chase before the heroes fell. He heard their strife on the hill; their song was soft, but sad. They mourned the fall of Morar, first of mortal men! His soul was like the soul of Fingal; his sword like the sword of Oscar. But he fell, and his father mourned; his sister's eyes were full of tears, the sister of car-borne Morar. She retired from the song of Ullin, like the moon in the west, when she foresees the shower, and hides her fair head in a cloud. I touched the harp with Ullin; the song of mourning rose!

"RYNO: The wind and the rain are past; calm is the noon of day. The clouds are divided in heaven. Over the green hills flies the inconstant sun. Red through the stony vale comes down the stream of the hill. Sweet are thy murmurs, O stream! but more sweet is the voice I hear. It is the voice of Alpin, the son of song, mourning for the dead! Bent is his head of age; red his tearful eye. Alpin, thou son of song, why alone on the silent hill? why complainest thou, as a blast in the wood, as a wave on the lonely shore?

"ALPIN: My tears, O Ryno! are for the dead—my voice for those that have passed away. Tall thou art on the hill; fair among the sons of the vale. But thou shalt fall like Morar; the mourner shall sit on thy tomb. The hills shall know thee no more; thy bow shall lie in thy hall unstrung!

"Thou wert swift, O Morar! as a roe on the desert; terrible as a meteor of fire. Thy wrath was as the storm; thy sword in battle as lightning in the field. Thy voice was a stream after rain, like thunder on distant hills. Many fell by thy arms: they were consumed in the flames of thy wrath. But when thou didst return from war, how peaceful was thy brow! Thy face was like the sun after rain, like the moon in the silence of night; calm as the breast of the lake when the loud wind is laid.

"Narrow is thy dwelling now! dark the place of thine abode! With three steps I compass thy grave, O thou who was so great before! Four stones, with their heads of moss, are the only memorial of thee. A tree with scarce a leaf, long grass which whistles in the wind, mark to the hunter's eye the grave of the mighty Morar. Morar! thou are low indeed. Thou hast no mother to mourn thee, no maid with her tears of love. Dead is she that brought thee forth. Fallen is the daughter of Morglan.

"Who on his staff is this? Who is this whose head is white with age, whose eyes are red with tears, who quakes at every step? It is thy father, O Morar! the father of no son but thee. He heard of thy fame in war, he heard of foes dispersed. He heard of Morar's renown; why did he not hear of his wound? Weep, thou father of Morar! Weep, but thy son heareth thee not. Deep is the sleep of the dead—low their pillow of dust. No more shall he hear thy voice—no more awake at thy call. When shall it be morn in the grave, to bid the slumberer awake? Farewell, thou bravest of men! thou conqueror in the field! But the field shall see thee no more, nor the dark wood be lightened with the splendor of thy steel. Thou hast left no son. The song shall preserve thy name. Future times shall hear of thee—they shall hear of the fallen Morar!

"The grief of all arose, but most the bursting sigh of Armin. He remembers the death of his son, who fell in the days of his youth. Carmor was near the hero, the chief of the echoing Galmal. Why burst the sigh of Armin? he said. Is there a cause to mourn? The song comes with its music to melt and please the soul. It is like soft mist that, rising from a lake, pours on the silent vale; the green flowers are filled with dew, but the sun returns in his strength, and the mist is gone. Why art thou sad, O Armin, chief of the sea-surrounded Gorma?

"Sad I am, nor small is my cause of woe! Carmor, thou hast lost no son, thou hast lost no daughter of beauty. Colgar the valiant lives, and Annira, fairest maid. The boughs of thy house ascend, O Carmor! But Armin is the last of his race. Dark is thy bed, O Daura! deep they sleep in the tomb! When shalt thou wake with thy songs—with all thy voice of music? Arise, winds of autumn, arise; blow along the heath! Streams of the mountains roar; roar, tempests in the groves of my oaks! Walk through broken clouds, O moon! show thy pale face at intervals; bring to my mind the night when all my children fell—when Arindal the mighty fell, when Daura the lovely failed. Daura, my daughter, thou wert fair —fair as the moon on Fura, white as the driven snow, sweet as the breathing gale. Arindal, thy bow was strong, thy spear was swift on the field, thy lock was like mist on the wave, thy shield a red cloud in a storm! Armar, renowned in war, came and sought Daura's love. He was not long refused: fair was the hope of their friends.

"Erath, son of Odgal, repined: his brother had been slain by Armar. He came disguised like a son of the sea; fair was his skiff on the wave, white his locks of age, calm his serious brow. Fairest of women, he said, lovely daughter of Armin! a rock not distant in the sea bears a tree on its side: red shines the fruit afar. There Armar waits for Daura. I come to carry his love! She went—she called on Armar. Naught answered but the son of the rock. Armar, my love, my love! why tormentest thou me with fear? Hear, son of Arnart, hear! it is Daura who calleth thee. Erath the traitor fled laughing to the land. She lifted up her voice—she called for her brother and her father. Arindal! Armin! none to relieve you, Daura.

"Her voice came over the sea. Arindal, my son, descended from the hill, rough in the spoils of the chase. His arrows rattled by his side; his bow was in his hand, five dark-gray dogs attended his steps. He saw fierce Erath on the shore; he seized and bound him to an oak. Thick wind the thongs of the hide around his limbs; he loads the winds with his groans. Arindal ascends the deep in his boat to bring Daura to land. Armar came in his wrath, and let fly the gray-feathered shaft. It sung, it sunk in thy heart. O Arindal, my son! for Erath the traitor thou diest. The oar is stopped at once: he panted on the rock and expired. What is thy grief, O Daura, when round thy feet is poured thy brother's blood? The boat is broken in twain. Armar plunges into the sea to rescue his Daura, or die. Sudden a blast from a hill came over the waves; he sank, and he rose no more.

"Alone, on the sea-beat rock, my daughter was heard to complain; frequent and loud were her cries. What could her father do? All night I stood on the shore: I saw her by the faint beam of the moon. All night I heard her cries. Loud was the wind; the rain beat hard on the hill. Before morning appeared, her voice was weak; it died away like the evening breeze among the grass of the rocks. Spent with grief, she expired, and left thee, Armin, alone. Gone is my strength in war, fallen my pride among women. When the storms aloft arise, when the north lifts the wave on high, I sit by the sounding shore, and look on the fatal rock. Often, by the setting moon, I see the ghosts of my children; half viewless they walk in mournful conference together."

A flood of tears which rushed from Lotte's eyes, giving relief to her oppressed heart, interrupted Werther's reading. He threw down the paper, took her hand, and broke into bitter sobs. Lotte rested her head on her arm and covered her eyes with her handkerchief. Both were in a terrible emotional state. They felt their own misery in the fate of the noble Gaels, felt it together and their tears mingled. Werther's lips and eyes burned on Lotte's arm, and a shudder ran through her body. She wanted to escape, but grief and pity weighed upon her with leaden force. She took a deep breath in order to control herself and, sobbing, asked Werther, in a lovely voice, to continue. Werther trembled; he thought his heart would break, but he took up the paper and read, his voice shaking with emotion:

"Why dost thou awake me, O breath of spring? Thou dost woo me and say: I cover thee with the dew of Heaven! But the time of my fading is near, near is the storm that will scatter my leaves! Tomorrow the wanderer shall come, he that saw me in my beauty shall come. His eyes will search me in the field around, and will not find me."

The whole power of these words rushed upon the unhappy man. Completely desperate, he threw himself at Lotte's feet, seized her hands, pressed them upon his eyes and against his forehead; and an apprehension of his terrible intention seemed to brush against her soul. A tumult rose in her; she took his hands, pressed them against her breast and, bending toward him with a mournful gesture, their glowing cheeks touched. The world was lost to them. He clasped her in his arms, held her close against him, and covered her trembling lips with a shower of passionate kisses. "Werther!" she cried with choking voice, turning away, "Werther!" She pushed him away with a feeble hand. "Werther!" she cried in a calmer tone, and with admirable dignity. He did not resist, released her from his embrace, and threw himself almost senseless on the floor at her feet. She quickly got up and said in a terrified confusion, torn between love and indignation, "This was the last time, Werther! You will not see me again." And with a look full of love for the unhappy man, she rushed into the next room and locked the door behind her. Werther stretched out his arms toward her but did not have the courage to hold her back. He lay on the floor, his head on the sofa, and remained in his position for more than half an hour, when a noise brought him to himself. It was the maid, who wanted to set the table. He walked up and down the room, and, when he saw that he was again alone, he went to the door of the next room and called gently, "Lotte! Lotte! only one word more! a farewell!" There was no answer. He waited and implored and again waited; then he rushed away, calling, "Farewell, Lotte! farewell forever!"

He came to the town gate. The watchman, who already knew him, opened it for him without a word. It drizzled between rain and snow; and a little before eleven he knocked at the gate again. His servant noticed, when Werther returned to his lodging, that his master had arrived hatless. He did not dare to mention this and helped him to undress; his clothes were wet through. His hat was later found on a steep bluff overlooking the valley, and it is hard to explain how he could have climbed to that height in the dark and wet night without falling to his death.

He went to bed and slept a long time. His servant found him writing when he brought the coffee he ordered the next morning. He was adding the following lines to his letter to Lotte:

"For the last time, then, for the last time I open my eyes to this world. Alas, they shall not see the sun again, for today it is hidden behind a veil of mist. Now, Nature, mourn your son, your friend, your lover who nears his end. Lotte, this is a unique sensation, and yet it resembles a twilight dream, when one says to oneself: 'This is the last morning. The last!' Lotte, these words mean nothing to me. Am I not standing here alive, in the possession of all my faculties, and yet tomorrow I shall lie prostrate and motionless on the ground. To die! What does that mean? Look, we are dreaming when we speak of death. I have seen many people die; but so limited is the human mind that it has no clear conception of the beginning and the end of our existence. At this moment I am still mine, yours! yours, my beloved! And the next moment— separated, divorced from you, perhaps forever? —No, Lotte, no! How can I *not* be? How can you *not* be? We *are* after all. —*Not* be! What does that mean? It is only a word, a mere sound, which stirs nothing in me. —Dead, Lotte! thrown into the cold ground, so narrow, so dark! —I once had a friend who meant everything to me in my awkward youth; she died, and I followed the bier and stood beside her grave when they lowered the coffin, and the ropes that held it whirred as they were loosened and jerked up again; and then the first shovelful of earth fell with a thud, and the fearful chest gave back a hollow sound, more muffled every time, until it was completely covered with earth. I fell to the ground beside the grave—shocked, shaken, frightened, heartbroken; but I did not know what had happened to me —what will happen to me. —Death! The grave! I do not understand these words.

"Oh, forgive me! forgive me! Yesterday! It should have been the last moment of my life. O angel! for the first time, quite without doubt, I had in my heart of hearts the glowing thought: she loves me! she loves me! My lips are still burning with the sacred fire kindled by yours; there is a fresh warm feeling of happiness in my heart. Forgive me! forgive me!

"Oh, I knew that you loved me—knew it from the first

warmhearted glance, from the first pressure of your hand; and yet, when I was not with you, when I saw Albert at your side, I was again tormented by feverish doubts.

"Do you remember the flowers you sent me when you had been unable to say one word to me or give me your hand at that hateful party? Oh, I was on my knees before them almost all night; and, for me, they put the seal on your love. But alas! these impressions faded, as the feeling of God's mercy gradually fades from the soul of the believer after it had been showered on him in holy and visible symbols.

"All this is transitory, but no Eternity shall extinguish the warm life that I drank yesterday from your lips and that I still feel within me. She loves me! This arm held her, these lips have trembled on her lips, this mouth has stammered against hers. She is mine! You are mine, Lotte, forever!

"And what does it mean that Albert is your husband? Husband! That may be for this world—and in this world it is sin that I love you, that I should like to snatch you from his arms into mine. Sin? Very well, and I am punishing myself for it; for this sin, which I have tasted in all its rapture, which gave me life-giving balm and strength. From now on you are mine! mine, Lotte! I go before you. I go to my Father, to your Father. I shall put my sorrow before Him, and He will comfort me until you come; and I shall fly to meet you and clasp you and stay with you before the Infinite Being in an eternal embrace.

"I do not dream; I am not deluded! So near to the grave, I see everything with great clearness. We shall be! we shall see one another again, see your mother. I shall see her, find her and ah! pour out all my heart to her, your mother, your very image."

Shortly before eleven o'clock Werther asked his servant if he thought Albert had returned. The boy said, "Yes, I saw his horse led into the stables." Werther then gave him an unsealed note which contained the words:

"Will you be good enough to lend me your pistols for my intended journey. And goodbye."

Lotte had slept little that night; everything she had feared had happened, in a manner which she had neither anticipated nor imagined. Her blood, that usually ran so innocently and lightly through her veins, was in a feverish tumult; a thousand emotions tormented her great soul. Was it the passion of Werther's embraces that reverberated in her heart? Was it indignation at his boldness? Was it a dissatisfied comparison of her present condition with those days of completely candid and frank innocence, when she had unclouded confidence in herself? How was she to face her husband? How to confess to him a scene which she might indeed describe without reserve, and yet of which she did not dare to make a clean breast? She and Albert had not talked to each other freely for so long. Should she now be the first to break silence and to give her husband such an unexpected disclosure just at the wrong time? She was afraid that even the mere mention of Werther's visit would make a disagreeable impression; and now this unexpected catastrophe! Was she allowed to hope that her husband would see the whole affair in the right light, would accept it entirely without prejudice? And could she wish him to read her heart? And yet, could she deceive the man in whose eyes she had always been like a crystal-clear glass—open and candid—and from whom she had been incapable of concealing any emotion, nor had wished to conceal any? All these questions worried her and made her uneasy; and all the while her thoughts kept returning to Werther, who was lost to her; whom she could not give up; whom she had, unfortunately, to leave to himself; and to whom, when he lost her, nothing was left.

How heavily the thought of the deadlock between Albert and herself weighed now on her heart, a deadlock which, at this moment, she could not explain. Even such sensible and good-natured people tend to become tongue-tied with each other, because of some latent differences of opinion; each of them thinking himself right and the other wrong; and the situation then becomes so complicated and exasperating that it is impossible to untie the knot at the critical moment on which all depends. If some happy intimacy had brought them together before this; if love and tolerance had mutually revived between them and opened their hearts—perhaps our friend might have been saved.

And yet, another strange circumstance played a part. Werther had never, as we know from his letters, kept his longing to depart from this world a secret. Albert had often argued with him on the subject; and this subject had several times been talked over by Lotte and her husband. The latter had not only felt a strong revulsion against such an act but also more than once said with a kind of irritability, which was otherwise quite incompatible with his character, that he believed he had sufficient reason to doubt the seriousness of any such intention on Werther's part; he had even sometimes allowed himself to ridicule the whole thing and mentioned his skeptical attitude to Lotte. This may have set her mind at rest for a time, whenever her thoughts presented to her the tragic picture—but it also prevented her from communicating to her husband the anxieties that tormented her at this moment.

Albert returned, and Lotte welcomed him with an embarrassed haste. He was not in a cheerful mood, as he had not been successful in settling his business, and the bailiff in the neighborhood had been a rigid, narrow-minded man. Besides, the roughness of the road had put him in a bad temper.

He asked if anything had happened, and she answered, much too quickly, "Werther was here last night." Then Albert asked if any letters had arrived, and was told that one letter and some packets had been put in his room. He went there, and Lotte was alone. The presence of the man whom she loved and respected had made a fresh impression upon her. She remembered his generosity, his love and his kindness, and felt more at ease. A secret impulse urged her to follow him; she took her needlework and went to his room as she often was in the habit of doing. She found him busy opening the packets and reading their contents. A few apparently contained rather unpleasant news. Lotte asked him several questions, which he answered curtly, and he then went to his high desk to write.

In this manner they passed an hour together, and Lotte's spirits were sinking lower and lower. She felt how difficult it would be for her to reveal to her husband, even if he were in the best of moods, all that weighed on her soul; and she lapsed into a sadness which distressed her only the more as she tried to hide it and choke down her tears.

When Werther's young servant appeared, she became very embarrassed. He handed the note to Albert, who calmly turned to his wife and said, "Give him the pistols!" —"I wish him a pleasant journey," he said to the youth. Lotte was thunderstruck; she staggered when she tried to get up, and almost fainted. Trembling, she walked slowly to the wall, took down the pistols, wiped off the dust, hesitated, and would have hesitated still longer if Albert's questioning glance had not urged her on. She gave the fatal weapons to the young man without saying a word; and when he had left the house, she gathered her work together and went to her room in a state of unspeakable anxiety. Her heart prophesied to her the most terrible possibilities. Her first thought was to throw herself at her husband's feet and to tell him the whole truth about last night's events, as well as her own guilt and her forebodings. But again she could not even hope to persuade her husband to go and see Werther. Meanwhile, the table had been set, and a good friend of Lotte's, who had stopped in for a moment to ask her something, said she would go immediately but stayed, making conversation during the meal more bearable. They pulled themselves together; they talked; they told stories, and were even able to forget.

The boy brought the pistols to Werther, who was delighted to hear that Lotte herself had handed them to him. He ordered bread and wine; then sent the boy out for his own supper, sat down and wrote:

"They have passed through your hands; you have wiped the dust from them. I kiss them a thousand times because you have touched them; and you, Heavenly Spirit, approve of my decision! And you, Lotte, offer me the weapon—you, from whose hands I wished to receive death, and ah! not receive it. Oh, how I questioned my servant! You trembled when you gave them to him, but you did not send me any farewell. Alas, alas! no farewell! Should you have closed your heart to me because of the moment that pledged me to you forever? Lotte, a thousand years cannot efface that memory! And I feel that you cannot hate him who burns with love for you."

After supper he told the boy to finish packing, tore up many papers, and went out to pay some small remaining debts. He returned and again went out, through the town gate, in spite of the rain, to the Count's garden. He wandered about the neighboring countryside, came back at nightfall and again wrote:

"Wilhelm, I have seen the fields, the woods, and the sky for the last time. Farewell, you, too! Dear Mother, forgive me! Comfort her, Wilhelm! God bless you both! My affairs are all settled. Farewell! We shall meet again and with more joy."

"Albert, I have repaid your kindness badly, and yet you will forgive me. I have disturbed the peace of your home; I have destroyed your confidence in each other. Farewell! I am about to make an end. Oh, if my death could make you happy again. Albert! Albert! Make the angel happy, and with this I implore God's blessing on you!"

In the evening he spent a great deal of time looking through his papers. He tore some up and threw them into the fire and sealed some packets addressed to Wilhelm. These contained short articles and fragmentary ideas, some of which I have read; and around ten o'clock, when he asked that the fire be replenished and that he be brought a bottle of wine, he sent his servant, whose room, like the other bedrooms of the house, was at the far end, to bed. The boy lay down without taking off his clothes so as to be ready at an early hour, for his master had told him that the post horses would be in front of the house before six o'clock the next morning.

"After eleven.

"Everything is so quiet around me, and my soul is so calm. I thank you, God, who gives these last moments such warmth, such strength! I walk to the window, my dearest, and see—still see—some stars in the eternal sky, shining through the stormy, fleeting clouds. No, you will not fall! The Eternal Father carries you near His heart, and me as well. I see the stars that make up the shaft of the Dipper, my favorite constellation. When I used to leave you at night and had passed your gate, these stars were just opposite me. How often have I looked up at them with rapture! How often have I raised my hands to them, regarding them as a symbol, a hallowed token of my happiness. And still now—O Lotte, does not everything remind me of you? Are you not always near me; and have I not, like a child, greedily snatched all sorts of trifles which you, dear saint, had touched!

"Precious silhouette! I return it to you, Lotte, and ask you to take good care of it. I have covered it with many, many kisses; I have greeted it a thousand times whenever I went out or came home.

"I have written your father a note and asked him to take care of my body. In the churchyard are two linden trees, in a far corner, next to the field; there I should like to rest. He can and will do this service to his friend. Do ask him, too. I do not like to hurt the feelings of devout Christians, who might not want to rest beside a poor, unhappy man. Oh, I wished you would bury me by the wayside or in a remote valley, where priest and Levite may pass by the marked stone, thankful that they are not as other men, and the Samaritan may shed a tear.

"Here, Lotte! I do not shudder to grasp the cold and dreadful cup from which I am about to drink the ecstasy of death. Your hand gave it to me, and I do not flinch. All, all the desires and hopes of my life are fulfilled! So cold, so rigid to knock at the iron gate of death.

"Had I been granted the happiness to die for *you!*, Lotte, to sacrifice myself for *you!* I would die bravely, I would die cheerfully, if I could restore to you the peace and happiness of your life. But alas! it is reserved for only a very few noble souls to shed their blood for those who are dear to them, and by their deaths to fan the flame of life of their friends to a new and wonderfully increased splendor.

"I want to be buried in these clothes I wear, Lotte! You have touched them and hallowed them. I have also asked your father to carry out this request. My soul hovers above the coffin. Do not let them look through my pockets. This rose-colored ribbon which you wore on your breast the first time I saw you, surrounded by your children—oh, give them a thousand kisses, and tell them the fate of their unhappy friend. The darling children! they swarm around me. Ah, how quickly I grew fond of you; I could not keep away from you from the first moment. —Let this ribbon be buried with me; you gave it to me on my birthday. How eagerly I accepted all this! —Ah, I did not think the way would end here! Be calm! Please, be calm!

"They are loaded. —The clock strikes twelve. —So be it! Lotte! Lotte! Farewell! Farewell!"

A neighbor saw the flash of the powder and heard the shot; but, as everything remained quiet, he did not pay further attention to it.

Next morning, around six o'clock, the servant entered the room with a candle. He found his master lying on the floor, the pistol beside him, and blood everywhere. He called, he touched him; no answer came, only a rattling in the throat. He ran for a doctor and for Albert. Lotte heard the bell; a tremor seized all her limbs. She woke her husband; they got up, and the servant, sobbing and stammering, told the news. Lotte fainted and fell to the ground at Albert's feet.

When the doctor arrived, he found the unfortunate young man on the floor, past help; his pulse was still beating; all his limbs were paralyzed. He had shot himself through the head above the right eye, and his brain was laid bare. They bled him needlessly; the blood flowed; he was still breathing.

From the blood on the back of the armchair they concluded that he had committed the act while sitting at his writing desk. He had then slid down and rolled around the chair in convulsions. He was lying on his back, facing the window, enfeebled, fully dressed, in his boots, his blue coat and yellow waistcoat.

The house, the neighborhood, the town, was in a tumult. Albert came in. They had laid Werther on his bed and bandaged his forehead; his face was already the face of a dead man; he did not move. His lungs still gave forth a dreadful rattling sound, now weak, now stronger; they expected the end.

He had drunk only one glass of the wine. Lessing's *Emilia Galotti* lay open on his desk.

I cannot describe Albert's consternation, Lotte's distress.

On hearing the news, the old bailiff rode up to the house at full speed; he kissed his dying friend and wept bitter tears. His older sons arrived soon afterward on foot; they knelt beside the bed with expressions of uncontrollable grief and kissed Werther's hands and mouth; the oldest, whom Werther had always loved most, clung to him to the bitter end, when they had to tear the boy away by force. Werther died at noon. The presence of the bailiff and the arrangements he made prevented a public disturbance. That night around eleven the bailiff had Werther buried at the place he himself had chosen. The old man and his sons followed the body to the grave; Albert was unable to. Lotte's life was in danger. Workmen carried the coffin. No clergyman attended.

Novella

At daybreak a thick autumn mist still flooded the spacious inner court of the Prince's castle; but when the veil gradually lifted, the hustle and bustle of the hunting party, on horseback and on foot, became more or less visible. The hurried preparations of those nearest at hand could be recognized: stirrups were lengthened or shortened, rifles and cartridge pouches passed around, knapsacks of badger skin adjusted, while the impatient hounds almost pulled their keepers along by their leashes. Here and there a horse pranced nervously, pricked by its own fiery temper or by the spur of its rider who, even in the dim light of the early morning, could not suppress a certain vanity to show off. All, however, were waiting for the Prince, whose farewells to his young wife had already caused too much delay.

Although those two had been married for only a short time, they already felt deeply the happiness of harmonious minds; both had active and lively dispositions and each enjoyed sharing the other's tastes and pursuits. The Prince's father had lived long enough to see, and to put to good use, the day when it became clear that all the members of a state should spend their lives in the same industrious way; that everyone should work and produce according to his faculties, should first earn and then enjoy his living.

How successful this policy had been became evident during these days when the great market was held, which might well be called a trade fair. The day before, the Prince had escorted his wife on horseback through the maze of piled-up merchandise and had drawn her attention to the favorable exchange of products here between the mountainous regions and the plain; he was able to demonstrate to her, at this very center, the industry of his own domain.

Although the Prince's conversation with his entourage had turned, during these days, almost exclusively upon these pressing topics, and although he was constantly conferring, in particular, with his Minister of Finance, yet the Master of the Hounds also carried his point when he made the tempting suggestion, impossible to resist, that he arrange a hunt—already once postponed—during these favorable autumn days, to give friends and the many guests, lately arrived, a special and rare treat.

The Princess was not very happy to be left behind; but the plan was to penetrate far into the mountains in order to harass the peaceful inhabitants of those forests by an unexpected invasion.

The Prince, at the moment of departure, did not forget to suggest that she should take a leisurely ride in the company of Prince Friedrich, his uncle. "And then," he added, "I also leave with you our Honorio as equerry and personal attendant. He will take care of everything." After saying these words he gave, on his way downstairs, the necessary instructions to a handsome young man; and then rode off with his guests and his attendants.

The Princess, after having waved her handkerchief to her husband in the courtyard below, went to the rooms on the other side of the castle, from which she had a clear view of the mountains—a view all the more beautiful since the rather elevated position of the castle above the river offered a variety of remarkable prospects on either side. She found the excellent telescope still in the position in which it had been left the evening before, when they had talked about the lofty ruins of the old family castle which could be seen over bush, mountain and wooded summit, and which had stood out unusually clear in the evening glow, the great masses of light and shade throwning into sharp relief this mighty monument of times long past. Now, in the early-morning light, the autumn colors of the various kinds of trees which had soared up unchecked and undisturbed through the masonry for so many years were startlingly distinct through the strong lenses which brought everything closer to the eye. The lovely lady, however, lowered the telescope slightly toward a barren stony tract where the hunting party would pass; she waited patiently for that moment and was not disappointed:

because of the clarity and magnifying power of the instrument, her bright eyes clearly recognized the Prince and the Grand Master of the Horse. She could not resist waving her handkerchief again when she more imagined than saw that they briefly halted and looked back.

At this moment Friedrich, the Prince's uncle, was announced. He entered the room with his draftsman who carried under his arm a large portfolio. "My dear niece," said the still-vigorous old gentleman, "we want to show you the drawings of the old castle, which have been made to demonstrate from various angles how remarkably well the powerful structure, built for shelter and defense, has resisted all seasons and all weathers from time immemorial, and how its masonry, nevertheless, has had to give way, here and there collapsing into desolate ruins. We have already taken steps to make this wilderness more accessible, for it is all that is needed to surprise and delight any wanderer or visitor."

After having explained to her in detail each single drawing, the old Prince continued: "Here, as we ascend through the hollow path in the outer ring of walls, we come to the castle itself, where a rock rises before us—one of the most massive rocks in the whole mountain range. Upon it a watchtower was built; but nobody would be able to say where nature ends and art and workmanship begin. Walls are annexed on both sides, and outworks slope downward in terraces. But this is not quite accurate, for it is actually a forest which girds this age-old summit. For the last hundred and fifty years no stroke of an ax has rung out here, and everywhere gigantic trees have grown to a great height. When you push your way along the walls, the smooth maple, the sturdy oak and the slender fir tree obstruct your progress with their trunks and roots, and you have to wind your way around them and choose your footing with caution. Look, how admirably has our masterly artist shown, in his drawing, these characteristic features; how clearly you can recognize the various kinds of trunk and root interwoven with the masonry, and the strong branches interlaced through the gaps in the walls. This wilderness has no parallel; it is a unique place, where ancient traces of long-vanished human strength can be seen in a deadly struggle with the everlasting and ever-acting forces of nature."

Taking up another drawing, he went on: "And what do you think of this courtyard, which became inaccessible after the collapse of the old gate tower and has never been entered by any human being for countless years! We tried to force an entrance from one side; we broke through walls, blasted vaults, and in this way made a convenient but secret passage. We did not have to clear up the inner court which is paved by a flat-topped rock made smooth by nature; but, even so, here and there huge trees have succeeded in anchoring their roots; they have grown up slowly but resolutely and are now thrusting their branches right up into the galleries where, once upon a time, knights paced up and down; they have become the true Lords and Masters, and Lords and Masters they may remain. After removing deep layers of dead leaves we discovered the most extraordinary level place, the like of which will probably not be found again in the whole world.

"We should, therefore, be grateful to our fine artist, whose various drawings have so convincingly reproduced the scene that we can imagine ourselves present. He has spent the best hours of the day and of the season on his work, and has studied these objects for weeks on end. On this corner we have arranged a small and pleasant lodging for him and the caretaker whom we have assigned to him. You cannot imagine, my dear, what a beautiful outlook and view into the open country and also toward the courtyard and ruins he can enjoy from there. But now, after sketching everything so neatly and faithfully, he will carry out his work down here at his convenience. We plan to decorate our garden room with these pictures, and no one will let his eyes wander over our symmetrically designed flowerbeds, our arbors and shady walks, without wishing to meditate in the castle itself, seeing both old things and new, that which is solid, inflexible and indestructible, and that which is vigorous, flexible and unresisting."

When Honorio entered and announced that the horses were ready, the Princess turned to her uncle and said: "Let us ride up there so that I can actually see everything you have shown me in these drawings. I have heard about that project ever since I came here; and now I feel a great desire to see with my own eyes what seemed to me impossible when described to me, and still unbelievable even after seeing the drawings."

"Not yet, my dear," replied the old Prince. "What you

have just seen is what it can and will be. At present some of the work has come to a standstill. Art must first complete its task, if it is not to be put to shame by nature."

"Then we'll at least ride in that direction, even if only to the foot of the crag. Today I am very much in the mood for having a look around far and wide."

"Just as you wish," answered the old Prince.

"But I should love to ride through the town," added the Princess, "across the great market place where all those booths give the illusion of a small town or a tented encampment. It is as though the needs and occupations of all the families round about were gathered at this central point and laid out to be seen in broad daylight; for the watchful observer can see here everything man produces and needs, and one can imagine for a moment that money is unnecessary, that any business can be transacted here by barter, which is also fundamentally true. After the Prince gave me an opportunity for this observation yesterday, I am pleased at the thought that in this place, where mountains border the plains, the people of both regions so clearly express what they need and want. Because the mountain dweller knows how to shape the wood of his forests into a hundred forms, and how to convert iron to any purpose, the plainsman comes here to meet him with goods of such great variety that one can often hardly recognize their material, nor guess the purpose they may serve."

"I know that my nephew takes a great interest in these matters," said the old Prince, "and just at this time of year it is most important to receive more than to spend; to accomplish this purpose is, ultimately, the sum of our whole state economy as well as of the smallest household budget. But forgive me, my dear, I never like to ride across a market place when a fair is going on; at every step obstacles block your way and stop you, and on such an occasion my imagination becomes kindled once more by the memory of that dreadful disaster which is branded, as it were, upon my eyes, when I saw similar piles of goods and merchandise go up in flames. I had scarcely—"

"Let us not waste these lovely morning hours," the Princess interrupted him, for the old gentleman had several times before frightened her by describing that catastrophe in detail, telling her how once, on a long journey, he had stopped at the best inn on a market place which was on that day packed with the commotion of a fair; how he had, in the evening, gone to bed, extremely tired, and had been roused during the night in a ghastly manner by screams and by flames that were rolling against his lodging.

The Princess hurried downstairs and mounted her favorite horse, but, instead of leaving through the back gate and riding uphill, she led her reluctantly willing companion through the front gate and downhill; for who would not be delighted to ride by her side, who would not have willingly followed her? Even Honorio, who had been looking forward to joining the hunters, had willingly stayed behind to devote himself entirely to her service.

As was to be expected, they could ride only step by step in the market place; but the lovely, gracious Princess cheered her companions with intelligent remarks whenever they were delayed. "I repeat my lesson of yesterday, for it is necessity that wishes to test our patience." And this was true, for the whole crowd pressed the riders so closely that they could move on only very slowly. The people were happy to catch a glimpse of the young lady, and many smiling faces showed definite pleasure in discovering that the first lady in the land was also the most beautiful and the most charming. There were mountain people, having come down from their quiet homes among rocks, firs and pines, and mixing with the plains people, who lived among hills, field and meadows; also tradespeople from small towns, and others who had assembled here. After having quietly surveyed the crowd, the Princess remarked to her companion how all these people, wherever they came from, used for their clothing more material than was necessary, more cloth and linen, more ribbon for trimming. "It seems to me that the women cannot pad themselves enough, nor the men puff themselves out enough to their satisfaction."

"And we won't begrudge them that pleasure," said the old gentleman. "People are happy, happiest indeed, when they can spend their surplus money on dressing themselves up and decking themselves out." The lovely lady nodded in agreement.

They had gradually advanced in this manner toward an

open square near the outskirts of the town, where they saw at the far end of a row of small booths and stalls a much larger wooden structure. Hardly had they sighted it when a deafening roar struck their ears. The feeding time for the wild animals on display there had evidently come; the lion raised his powerful forest-and-desert voice; the horses trembled; and one could hardly fail to realize the terrifying manner in which the King of the Desert announced his presence in the midst of the peaceful existence and pursuits of the civilized world. As they approached the building they could not help but see the huge, garish posters which represented in strong colors and striking images those strange animals and were meant to fill the peaceable citizen with an irresistible desire to see the show. A fierce, formidable tiger was seen attacking a blackamoor, about to tear him to pieces; a gravely majestic lion did not seem to see any prey worthy of his dignity; beside these mighty beasts, other strange and colorful creatures deserved less attention.

"On our way back," said the Princess, "let's dismount and have a closer look at these unusual guests."

"It is quite remarkable that human beings always want to be excited by something horrifying," said the old Prince. "In there, the tiger lies quietly in his cage, while out here he must make a furious leap on the blackamoor to make you believe that you will see him do the same within. As if there were not enough murder and bloodshed, fire and destruction in the world! The ballad singers have to repeat all this at every street corner. The good people want to be intimidated, so that they can afterwards feel, all the more intensely, how pleasant and relaxing it is to breathe freely."

Whatever uneasy feelings those alarming pictures may have given them, these were at once blotted out when they passed through the town gate into a perfectly serene countryside. They rode at first along the river, which was here still a rivulet, fit only for the traffic of small craft, but which farther on gradually widened to become one of the largest streams, retaining its name and bringing prosperity to distant countries. The gently rising road then led them through well-tended fruit and pleasure gardens, until a densely populated region gradually opened before them where, after having passed first a thicket and then a grove, charming villages limited but refreshed their view. A green valley, leading uphill, was a welcome change for the riders, as the grass had been lately mown for the second time, making the turf look like velvet; it was watered by a lively spring which came gushing down from some higher place. They now rode on to a higher and more open viewpoint which they reached, coming out of a wood, after a brisk ascent. It was then that they saw, though still at a considerable distance and over other groups of trees, the object of their pilgrimage—the old castle, rising aloft like the peak of some wooded crag. But when they turned around—and nobody arrived at this point without looking back—they saw to the left, through occasional gaps in the tall trees, the Prince's new castle, illuminated by the morning sun, the well-built upper part of the town, slightly obscured by light clouds of smoke, and farther to the right the lower town, the river with some of its windings, its meadowlands and gristmills, while straight before them extended a wide, fertile region.

After they had feasted their eyes on the beautiful panorama, or rather, as usually happens when we look about us from such a height, were feeling a strong desire for an even wider and unbounded view, they rode uphill on a broad and stony tract, with the mighty ruin facing them like a green-crested pinnacle with only a few old trees deep down at its foot. Riding through these trees, they found themselves confronted with the steepest, most inaccessible flank where enormous, age-old rocks, untouched by change, massive and firm, towered above. Between them huge stone slabs and fragments, tumbled down in the course of time, were lying across each other in confusion and seemed to forbid even the boldest climber to advance. But anything precipitous and abrupt seems to appeal to youth. To dare, to attack, to conquer is a delight for young limbs. The Princess indicated that she would like to make the attempt; Honorio was at hand, and the old gentleman, though not so enterprising, did not protest, being reluctant to confess to lesser energy. They decided to leave the horses below under the trees and to try and reach a certain point where an enormous projecting rock presented a level space from which they would have a view, almost a bird's-eye view, of scenery still picturesque, though slowly receding into the distance.

The sun, almost at its highest point, shed a brilliant light on everything: the new castle with its various parts, the main buildings, the wings, cupolas and towers looked very impressive. The upper part of the town could be seen in its full extent; they could even easily look into the lower town and, through the telescope, recognize the different stalls in the market place. It was Honorio's habit to carry this useful instrument with him, strapped over his shoulder. They looked up and down the river, where the land on this side was broken by mountainous terraces; on the other side was an undulating, fertile plain, alternating with moderate hills and innumerable villages—it was an old custom to argue how many could be counted from this spot.

Over this vast expanse reigned a serene stillness, as is usual at noon when Pan is sleeping, as the ancients said, and all nature is holding its breath for fear of wakening him.

"It is not for the first time," said the Princess, "that, standing on such a high place with a view in all directions, I have thought how pure and peaceful nature looks on a clear day, giving the impression that there could be nothing unpleasant in the world; but when we return into the habitations of human beings, be they high or low, large or small—there is always something to fight over, to dispute, to straighten out and set right."

Honorio, who had meanwhile been looking across at the town through the telescope, suddenly exclaimed: "Look! Look! A fire has started in the market place!" The others also looked and noticed some smoke, but the sunlight subdued the flames. "The fire is spreading!" all cried, looking by turns through the lenses; the good eyes of the Princess could now recognize the disaster even without the help of the instrument. Now and then they could perceive red tongues of flames; smoke rose up, and the old Prince suggested: "Let's ride back, this is bad; I have always been afraid that I might have this unfortunate experience a second time." When they had climbed down and had reached their horses, the Princess turned to her uncle. "Please, ride back quickly, and take your groom with you. Leave Honorio with me; we'll follow at once." Her uncle, feeling that her suggestion was as reasonable as it was necessary, rode down the rough, stony slope as quickly as the condition of the ground allowed.

When the Princess had mounted her horse, Honorio said: "I implore Your Highness to ride slowly! Both in the town and at the castle everything for fighting fires is in the best order and nobody will lose his head in such an unusual and unexpected emergency. But the road here is bad, small stones and short grass, to ride fast is unsafe; in any case, the fire will certainly have been put out by the time we arrive." The Princess did not believe this. She saw the smoke spreading; she thought she saw a blazing flame and heard an explosion; and now all the terrifying scenes of the fire at the fair, witnessed by her uncle and described to her repeatedly, were evoked in her imagination on which they were unfortunately impressed all too deeply.

That former incident had been terrible, unexpected and shocking enough to leave behind a lifelong impression as well as an anxious apprehension of a possible recurrence of that kind of disaster. In the dead of night a sudden blaze had

seized stall after stall on the great crowded market place,
even before the people who were sleeping in or near those
flimsy booths had been shaken from their dreams. The old
Prince, a stranger, tired after a long journey, had retired
early but, wakened from his first sleep, he had rushed to the
window to see the ghastly illumination, flame upon flame,
darting on every side and licking fiery tongues toward him.
The houses on the market place, tinted red by the reflection,
seemed to glow, threatening to catch fire at any moment and
to burst into flames; below, the irresistible element kept raging, the boards crashed to the ground, laths cracked, pieces
of tent canvas flew up, and the tatters, blackened and with
jagged and flaming edges, reeled in the air, as if evil spirits,
shaped and reshaped by their element, would consume
themselves in a playful round dance, trying to emerge now
and then out of the flames. Meanwhile, with piercing
screams, people were saving whatever they could take hold
of; servants and hired men helped their masters to drag to
safety bales of goods already on fire, to snatch at least something from the racks and stuff it into the crates, although
they were forced in the end to abandon everything to the
destruction of the swiftly advancing flames. How many,
wishing that the roaring fire would stop for a moment, had
looked around for a possible breathing space and been seized
by the flames with all their possessions. Everything that
smoldered or was burning on the one side lay on the other
still in deep darkness. Determined characters, men with a
strong will, fiercely fought their fiery adversary and saved a

few things, though they lost their hair and their eyebrows. It was unfortunate that the wild confusion of that past event was now evoked again in the pure mind of the Princess. The serene horizon of the morning seemed suddenly clouded, her eyes dimmed, and even wood and meadow took on a strangely ominous look.

Riding into the peaceful valley, but oblivious to its refreshing coolness, they had hardly passed the lively source of the stream, flowing nearby, when the Princess caught sight of something unusual far below in the bushes of the meadowland, which she at once recognized as the tiger; leaping, it came up toward them, just as she had seen it on the poster a short time ago, and its sudden appearance, adding to the terrifying scenes which occupied her mind at this moment, affected her very strongly. "Flee, Madam!" shouted Honorio, "flee at once!" She turned her horse and rode up the steep hill from which they had just descended. But the young man rode toward the beast, drew his pistol and, when he thought he was within range, fired; but, unfortunately, he missed his mark. The tiger jumped aside, Honorio's horse shied, and the enraged animal continued on its way upward, closely following the Princess. She raced her horse as fast as it would go up the steep and stony slope, forgetting for the moment that the gentle creature, unaccustomed to such efforts, might not stand the strain. Urged on by its hard-pressed rider, the horse overtaxed itself, stumbled now and then over the loose stones of the slope and, after one last violent effort, fell exhausted to the ground. The lovely lady, resolute and expert, managed to get quickly to her feet; the horse, too, scrambled up, but the tiger was coming nearer, although at a slower pace; the rough ground and the sharp stones seemed to check its progress, and only the fact that Honorio was in close pursuit appeared to irritate and goad it on again. Racing toward the place where the Princess was standing beside her horse, both runners arrived at the same time. The chivalrous young man leaned from his horse, fired his second pistol, and shot the beast through the head. The tiger fell at once and, stretched out at full length, showed more clearly than ever its tremendous power, the physical frame of which was now all that was left. Honorio had jumped from his horse and knelt on the animal, stifling any last sign of life, his drawn hunting knife ready in his right hand. He was a handsome youth whom the Princess had often before seen galloping his horse, as he had just now, at the tournaments. In the same way, while riding in the manège at a full gallop, his bullet had hit the Turk's head (mounted on a pole) right under the turban; and again, approaching at an easy gallop, he had speared the Moor's head from the ground with the point of his drawn sword. In all such arts he was skilled and lucky, and both skill and luck had now stood him in good stead.

"Give it the finishing stroke!" cried the Princess. "I'm afraid the beast may still hurt you with its claws."

"Excuse me, but it is already dead," the young man answered, "and I do not want to spoil its pelt which shall adorn your sledge next winter."

"Don't be frivolous at a moment like this, which calls forth all feelings of reverence in the depth of our hearts," said the Princess.

"I too have never in my life felt more reverence than at this moment," exclaimed Honorio, "but just for that reason I think of something cheerful and can look at this pelt only in the light of your future pleasure."

"It would always remind me of this dreadful moment," she replied.

"But isn't it a much more innocent trophy than the weapons of defeated enemies which used to be carried in the triumphal procession before a conqueror?" asked the young man with glowing cheeks.

"I shall always remember your courage and skill when I look at it; and I need not add that you can count on my gratitude and the Prince's favor as long as you live. But do stand up now! There is no longer any life in the beast, and we must think of what to do next. First of all, stand up!"

"Since I am already on my knees before you, in an attitude which would be forbidden to me in any other circumstances, I beg of you to give me at once a proof of the kindness and good will which you just promised me," said the young man. "I have asked your husband, the Prince, several times before to give me leave and the permission to go abroad. Any person who has the good fortune to sit at your table and have the privilege of your company should have seen the world. Persons who have traveled widely come here from all parts, and as soon as the conversation turns to a certain town or any place of importance in some part of the world, we are asked if we have been there. No one who has not seen all these things is considered an educated person; it seems as if we should inform ourselves only for the benefit of others."

"Stand up!" the Princess said once more. "I do not like to ask my husband for anything that runs contrary to his opinions; but if I am not mistaken, the reason why he has kept you here until now will soon be removed. His intention was to see you matured into an independent nobleman who would do credit both to himself and to his Prince when abroad as he did here; and I should think that your action today would be the best letter of recommendation a young man could carry with him into the world."

The Princess did not have time to notice that a shadow of sadness rather than youthful delight passed over Honorio's face; nor did he himself have time to give way to his feelings, for a woman, holding a boy by the hand, came running in great haste up to where they were standing; and hardly had Honorio collected himself and got up, when she flung herself, weeping and crying, on the lifeless body of the tiger. Her behavior as well as her picturesque and odd, though clean and decent, dress showed that she was the owner and keeper of the creature stretched on the ground. The dark-eyed boy with curly dark hair, holding a flute in his hand, knelt down beside his mother and also wept with deep feeling, although less violently.

This unhappy woman's wild outburst of passion was followed by a stream of words which, though incoherent and fitful, flowed like a brook gushing from one rocky ledge to another. This natural language, short and abrupt, was most impressive and touching. As it would be impossible to try and translate her words into our idiom, we can give only an approximate meaning.

"They have murdered you, poor creature! murdered you needlessly! You were tame and would have loved to lie down quietly and wait for us, for your pads hurt you and your claws had no strength left. You missed the hot sun, which would have made them grow strong. You were the most beautiful of your kind; no man ever saw a royal tiger, so splendidly stretched out in sleep, as you lie now, dead, never to rise again! When, in the morning, you woke at daybreak, opened your jaws wide and put out your red tongue, you seemed to smile at us; and even though you roared, you still took your food playfully from the hands of a woman, from the fingers of a child! How long we traveled with you on your journeys; how long was your company important and rewarding to us! To us, yes, to us it came true: 'Out of the eater came forth meat, and out of the strong came forth sweetness.' All this is now over! Alas, alas!"

Her lament was not yet finished when riders came down the slope from the castle, galloping at full speed. They were soon recognized as the hunting party, headed by the Prince himself. While hunting in the mountains beyond, they had seen the smoke clouds rising from the fire and had taken a direct path toward these ominous signs, racing through valleys and gorges as if in eager pursuit of game. Galloping over the stony ground, they now stopped short and stared at the unexpected group, which stood out with remarkable distinctiveness on the level clearing. After the first recognition nobody spoke a word, and when everyone had somewhat recovered from the surprise, a few words were sufficient to explain what had not been obvious at a first glance. As he heard about the extraordinary and unheard-of occurrence, the Prince stood among his attendants on horseback and the men who had hurried after him on foot. There was no doubt about what to do; the Prince gave his orders and instructions, when suddenly a tall man forced his way into the circle. He was dressed in the same strange and colorful fashion as his wife and child. And now the whole family was united in mutual surprise and grief. The man, however, collected himself and, standing at a respectful distance from the Prince, said to him: "This is not a moment for lament. Oh, my lord and mighty hunter, the lion too is at large and has come to these hills, but spare him, have pity and let him not be killed like this good animal here."

"The lion?" said the Prince. "Have you found his tracks?"

"Yes, my lord! A peasant in the valley who needlessly took refuge in a tree directed me to go up this hill to the left; but when I saw the crowd of men and horses I hurried here, being curious and in need of help."

"Then the hunt must start in that direction," the Prince ordered. "Load your guns; go cautiously to work. It will do no harm if you drive the animal into the woods below; but in the end, my good man, we won't be able to spare your favorite creature. Why have you been so careless as to let both animals escape?"

"The fire broke out," the man replied. "We kept quiet and waited to see what would happen. It spread very fast but was far away. We had enough water to protect ourselves, but some gunpowder exploded, and burning fragments were blown over to us and beyond. We left in haste and confusion and are now very unhappy people."

The Prince was still busy giving instructions, but for a moment everything seemed to come to a standstill, for a man was seen running down from the old castle—a man they soon recognized to be the castellan who was in charge of the painter's workroom where he lived, being also the supervisor of the workmen. He arrived out of breath, but quickly told his story in a few words: behind the upper rampart the lion had peacefully settled down in the sunshine, at the foot of a hundred-year-old beech tree. But the castellan angrily concluded: "Why did I take my gun to town yesterday to have it cleaned! If I had had it handy, the lion would not have stood up again; the skin would be mine, and I would have bragged about it all my life, and justly so!"

The Prince, whose military experience was now of value to him, for he had found himself before in situations where inevitable trouble had threatened from several sides, turned to the first man, saying: "What guarantees can you give me that your lion, should we spare him, will do no harm to my people in this region?"

"My wife and my child offer to tame him, and to keep him

quiet until I have managed to bring up here the iron-barred cage in which we'll take him back again, harmless and unharmed," answered the father hastily.

The boy evidently wished to try out his flute, an instrument of the kind formerly called "flauto dolce," which had a short mouthpiece like a pipe. Those who know how to play it can produce the most pleasant sounds. Meanwhile, the Prince had asked the castellan how the lion had managed to enter the castle grounds. The man answered: "By the narrow passage which is walled in on both sides and has, for ages, been the only approach and is meant to remain so. Two footpaths, formerly leading up, have been so completely obstructed that, except by this narrow approach, no one can enter the magic castle which the mind and taste of Prince Friedrich intended it to become."

After some moments of reflection, watching the child who all the time had been playing softly his flute as if preluding, the Prince turned to Honorio, saying: "You have accomplished much today, finish now what you began. Take some men with you and hold the narrow passage, have your guns ready but do not shoot unless you cannot drive back the beast in any other manner. If necessary, build a fire to scare it if it should try to come down. This man and his wife may take responsibility for the rest." Honorio at once set about carrying out these orders.

The child went on playing his tune, which was actually only a sequence of notes without any precise order and perhaps for this very reason was so deeply moving. Those standing around seemed to be under the spell of the melodious rhythm, when the father of the boy began to speak with appropriate enthusiasm:

"God has given the Prince wisdom and also the knowledge that all the works of God are wise, each in its own way. Look at that rock, how firm it stands; it does not move and braves the storms and the sunshine. Ancient trees surround its summit, and proudly it looks around far and wide. If one of its parts should crumble, it does not want to remain where it was but falls down, shattered to pieces, and covers the side of the slope. But even there the pieces will not stay; playfully they leap into the depth below; the brook receives them and carries them to the river. Neither resisting nor obstinate and angular, but smooth and rounded, they move along with increasing speed and pass from river to river, till they finally reach the ocean, where a host of giants are marching and the deep is swarming with dwarfs.

"But who sings the glory of the Lord, whom the stars praise for ever and ever? And why do you look in distant places? Look at the bees! Late in the fall they are still harvesting and build themselves a house, true and level, at once masters and workmen. Watch the ants: they know their way and never lose it; they build themselves a home of grass, crumbs of earth and pine needles; they build it up and cover it with a vaulted roof; but they have worked in vain, for the horse paws the ground and destroys everything. Look! it crushes their rafters and scatters their planks; it snorts impatiently and is restless; for the Lord has made the horse a brother to the wind and a companion of the storms, to carry man wherever he wishes, and woman wherever she desires to go. But in the palm grove the lion appeared. At a dignified pace he crossed the desert, where he reigns over all the other animals and nothing withstands him. Yet man knows how to tame him, and the cruellest of creatures has respect for him, the image of God, in which the angels too are made who serve the Lord and His servants. For in the lion's den Daniel was not afraid; he stood firm and was confident, and the wild roaring did not interrupt his hymn of praise."

This speech, delivered with an expression of natural enthusiasm, the child accompanied with occasional melodious sounds on his flute; but when his father had finished, the boy began to sing in a clear, ringing voice, with skillful modulations, whereupon the father took the flute and accompanied the child, who sang:

> From the deep and from the darkness
> Rises now the prophet's song;
> God and Angels hover round him—
> Why should he fear wrong?
> Lion and lioness together
> Rub against his knees and purr,
> For that melting holy music
> Stills their savage stir.

The father continued to accompany each strophe on the flute, while the mother joined in, from time to time, as a second voice. But it was particularly moving when the child began to change the order of the lines of the verse; and even though he did not give a new meaning to the whole, he intensified his own feeling and the feelings of the listeners.

> Round the child those Angels hover
> Guarding him with sacred song;
> In the deep and in the darkness
> Why should he fear wrong?
> In the presence of that music
> Never may misfortune dwell;
> Round my path the Angels hover:
> All things shall be well.

All three then sang together with force and exaltation:

> For the Eternal rules the waters,
> Rules the earth, the air, the fire;
> Like a lamb the lion shall gambol
> And the flood retire.
> Lo! the naked sword of anger
> Hangs arrested in midair:
> Strong the Love and great its wonders
> That abides in prayer.

All were silent; all heard and listened; and only when the sounds had died away could one notice and observe the general impression. Everyone seemed to have calmed down; everyone was touched in a different manner. The Prince, as if he only now realized the disaster which had threatened him a short time ago, looked down at his wife, who was leaning against him and was not ashamed to take her small embroidered handkerchief and press it to her eyes. It did her good to feel her youthful heart relieved of the oppression that had weighed on it during the last hour. Complete silence reigned in the crowd; all seemed to have forgotten the dangers around them: the fire in the town below and, from above, the possible appearance of a suspiciously quiet lion.

The Prince was the first to get the crowd moving again when he gave the order to lead the horses nearer. Then he turned to the woman and said: "Do you really believe that you can attract and tame the escaped lion, wherever you find him, by your singing and the sounds of your child's flute, and that you can take him back under lock and key without harm to others and to the beast itself?" They assured him that they could certainly do this, whereupon the castellan was appointed to be their guide. The Prince now left hurriedly with a few of his men, while the Princess followed more slowly with the others; but the mother and her son, accompanied by the castellan, who had meanwhile armed himself with a gun, climbed up the steep slope.

At the entrance to the narrow passage, the only approach to the old castle, they found the huntsmen busily piling up dry brushwood to build, if necessary, a large fire.

"It will not be necessary," said the woman. "Everything will be done in a friendly manner."

Farther on they saw Honorio sitting on a spur of the wall, his double-barreled gun across his knees, like a sentry prepared for anything that might happen. But he hardly seemed to notice them as they approached. He sat there as if sunk deep in thoughts and looked around in an absent-minded way. The woman spoke to him, imploring him not to let his men light the fire, but he seemed to give little attention to what she said; she went on to speak with great animation and exclaimed: "Handsome young man, you killed my tiger —I do not curse you. Spare my lion, good young man, and I shall bless you."

But Honorio looked straight ahead at the sun, which was slowly going down.

"You look westward," the woman cried, "and that is well, for there is much to be done there. But hurry, do not delay! You will conquer. But first conquer yourself!" At this, Honorio seemed to smile; the woman continued on her way but could not refrain from looking back once more at the young man; the red glow of the sun flushed his face, and she thought she had never seen a more handsome youth.

"If your child," said the castellan, "can really charm and quiet the lion with his song and his flute, as you are convinced he can, we shall quite easily subdue the powerful beast, for it has settled down quite close to the vaults through which we have broken an entrance into the courtyard, since the main gate has been blocked up by ruins. If the child can lure the lion in there, I can close the opening without any difficulty, and the boy can, if he wants, escape from the animal over one of the narrow winding stairs which he can see in the corners. We two are going to hide; but I shall take up a position from where my bullet can come to the child's aid at any moment."

"All these preparations are unnecessary. God and our own skill, faith and good fortune are our best aides."

"That may be so," said the castellan, "but I know my duty. First I shall lead you by a difficult ascent up to the battlements just opposite the entrance I mentioned before. Your child may descend then, as it were, into the arena of a theater and lure the trusting beast into it."

And so it happened: from their hiding place above, the castellan and the mother saw the child walking down the winding stairs into the bright courtyard, and then disappearing into the dark opening opposite; but they could immediately hear the sounds of his flute which gradually died away and finally stopped. The silence was ominous enough; the old hunter, though familiar with danger, felt ill at ease in this strange case concerning a human being. He thought to himself that he would prefer to face the dangerous animal himself; the mother, however, with a cheerful face, leaned far over the parapet and listened, not showing the slightest sign of uneasiness.

At last they heard the flute again; with eyes radiant with joy the child came out of the dark vault, the lion following him slowly and apparently walking with some difficulty. Now and then the animal seemed inclined to lie down, but the boy led it around in a half circle among the trees, which still showed some of their bright autumn foliage. Finally he sat down, almost transfigured by the last rays of the sun shining through a gap in the ruins, and began once more his soothing song, which we cannot refrain from repeating:

> From the deep and from the darkness
> Rises now the prophet's song;

> God and Angels hover round him—
> >   Why should he fear wrong?
> > Lion and lioness together
> > Rub against his knees and purr,
> > For that melting holy music
> >   Stills their savage stir.

The lion had meanwhile nestled close to him, placing his heavy right forepaw in the lap of the boy, who, continuing to sing, stroked it gently but soon noticed that a sharp thorn was stuck between the pads. Carefully removing the painful point, the boy took off his bright-colored scarf with a smile and bandaged the fearful paw, so that his mother, leaning back, flung up her arms in delight and would probably have applauded—clapping her hands in the usual manner—had not a firm grip of the castellan's fist reminded her that the danger was not yet over.

After playing a few notes on the flute as a prelude, the child sang triumphantly:

> For the Eternal rules the waters,
> Rules the earth, the air, the fire;
> Like a lamb the lion shall gambol
>   And the flood retire.
> Lo! the naked sword of anger
> Hangs arrested in midair:
> Strong the Love and great its wonders
>   That abides in prayer.

If it is possible to believe that an expression of friendliness, of grateful satisfaction, can be perceived on the features of such a fierce creature, the tyrant of the forests, the despot of the animal kingdom, then here it was seen; for the child, in his transfiguration, seemed really like a powerful and victorious conqueror, and the lion, though not looking like a defeated being, for his strength was only for a time concealed, did yet seem a tamed being, having surrendered to his own peaceable will. The child went on playing the flute and singing, transposing the verses and adding new ones in his own way:

> So good children find the Angels
> Near them in their hour of need,
> To prevent designing evil
> And promote the shining deed.
> So the dear child walks in safety,
> For the notes, bewitching sweet,
> Bring the tyrant of the forest
> Gentle to his gentle feet.

About the Author

JOHANN WOLFGANG VON GOETHE was born in Frankfurt in 1749. He completed a law degree while also writing his first lyric poems and pursuing his interest in the study of biological morphology.

Goethe's novel *The Sorrows of Young Werther,* written in 1774, made him famous. In 1775 he was invited to the court of the Duke of Saxe-Weimar, where he lived for the rest of his life. There he was minister of state for ten years and director of the state theater. The publication of *Wilhelm Meister* and *Faust* helped to make Goethe a literary legend in his own lifetime. He spoke seven languages, wrote on acoustics, and was an accomplished musician. When he died, in 1832, he was buried next to Schiller in the ducal crypt at Weimar.

VINTAGE FICTION, POETRY, AND PLAYS

VINTAGE BIOGRAPHY AND AUTOBIOGRAPHY